The

Newspaper Club

THE CUBS GET
THE SCOOP

BETH VRABEL

Illustrated by Paula Franco

RP|KIDS
PHILADELPHIA

Running Press Kids
Hachette Book Group
1290 Avenue of the Americas, New York, NY 10104
www.runningpress.com/rpkids
@RP_Kids

Printed in the United States   .

First Edition: September 2020

Published by Running Press Kids, an imprint of Perseus Books, LLC,
a subsidiary of Hachette Book Group, Inc. The Running Press Kids name
and logo is a trademark of the Hachette Book Group.

The Hachette Speakers Bureau provides a wide range of authors for speaking events.
To find out more, go to www.hachettespeakersbureau.com or call (866) 376-6591.

Print book cover and interior design by Marissa Raybuck.

Library of Congress Control Number: 2019953740

ISBNs: 978-0-7624-9688-4 (hardcover),
978-0-7624-9691-4 (ebook)

LSC-C

10   9   8   7   6   5   4   3   2   1

TO MOM AND DAD, WHO MODELED
READING A NEWSPAPER EVERY NIGHT

CHAPTER ONE

I CLAPPED TO GET the attention of the news staff. They were too busy chatting with each other or feeding Stuff (the goat) to pay attention to their editor (me).

"All right, guys. We have three weeks until school starts. Just enough time to release another issue. What's on the **budget**?"

"Budget?" Thom was sitting on a hay bale next to Stuff. Technically speaking, this newsroom was Thom's barn.

"Newspaper budgets don't have anything to do with money," I explained. "It's a breakdown of the stories that we're planning—or budgeting for—in the next issue."

"But what about the other kind of budget? Are walkie talkies in that budget?" Min asked as she pulled the ruffles of her dress out of Stuff's mouth. Min lived next to me and across the street from Thom, wore ruffles on every outfit, and was prone to dotting the *i* in her name with a heart.

"I do *not* have money for this," Gloria said. She crossed her thin arms and narrowed her eyes. Gloria was wearing the blue jersey-style uniform shirt from her shift at Wells Diner, the restaurant downtown her dad owned. "No one said we needed money to be on the newspaper."

"None of us have money," I pointed out. We lived in Bear Creek, Maine. Think of a super-hip neighborhood in a city and then make everything the total opposite. That's Bear Creek. No one is rich, but Min's family comes close. Her whole family—grandparents, aunts and uncles, cousins—goes to Disney World every summer. This year, her aunties from Korea joined them, too. (Even her dad had been wearing mouse ears when they got back from the airport last week. My dad would never do that. *It's called dignity,* I heard his voice in my mind. But I knew that I was just expressing my thoughts in his voice. The truth is, Dad totally would've worn mouse ears. But he would've also pointed out that commercial vacations were an indulgence that shouldn't be repeated.)

I cleared my throat. "We don't have a budget about money, just articles we're planning. Besides, we don't need walkie talkies, Min. We all have cell phones."

"Walkie talkies are more fun." Min crossed her arms.

"Oh," Gloria said. "I'm okay with story budgets." Her long brown hair was braided in cornrows except for her bangs, which she blew off her forehead with a puff. The purple and silver beads at the ends of her braids clicked when she shrugged.

Gordon pushed off the hay bale next to Gloria and leaned against the side of the barn, looking out the door over Thom's yard. His mom, Dr. Burke, was the superintendent of Bear Creek School District. Dr. Burke and Gordon were a lot alike, and not just because of their looks (both had wide smiles, brown skin, and freckles). They also had something about them that made people around them sit up and take notice. Dad would call them charismatic. I bet Gordon's family didn't worry about going on vacation, either. They had a red brick house in Foxcroft Estates, the part of town where people hired landscapers to mow their lawn into long stripes. Mrs. Kim-Franklin told Mom they'd live there but the homes "lacked character." (I think she just wanted to let people know that the Kim-Franklins could afford fancy grass.)

"I have money," Min said, as though she had read my thoughts. At ten, Min is younger than the rest of us, which might explain her affinity for ruffles and pastel colors. I am almost twelve. I wear black and gray as a matter of principle.

Right then Min was wearing a lavender sundress with a ruffle across the chest. She also wore white sneakers with, you guessed it, white ruffled socks. Even her purple headband was ruffled where it lay against her dark hair. Min opened the small mouse-eared backpack resting by her feet and pulled out a twenty-dollar bill. Waving it in the air, she said, "I got allowance last night. Why don't we go to the creamery?"

"You got back from vacation a couple days ago," I said. "How could you've possibly earned an allowance?"

Min shrugged. "I get paid every Monday."

"For what?"

"For being a kid."

I once pulled every weed in the flower gardens surrounding our old farmhouse—even got scraped on the huge yellow rosebush by the front door—and all I got was a ten-dollar bill from Mom.

"Do you want ice cream or not?" Min asked.

"Of course I want ice cream," I snarled. Everyone jumped to their feet, even Charlotte, who had been sitting in a shadowy corner of the barn reading the *AP Stylebook* like the dream copy editor she was.

"Wait!" I held up my hand to stop them. "We don't have time for ice cream right now. We have to figure out the next issue."

"Well, we have the Annabelle story," Thom pointed out. He must've noticed Gloria blowing on her forehead because he turned on an old metal fan in the corner of the barn. Stuff rammed forward and stood directly in front of the breeze, emitting goat-scented air throughout the barn. Charlotte leaned over and unplugged the fan, making everyone laugh. Soon Charlotte's face was as red as her hair. She was super quiet; even after weeks of hanging out in the barn—I mean newsroom—I still didn't know her well.

I sighed. Annabelle lived a couple blocks from the newsroom in a little Cape Cod house where everything looked even neater and cleaner than at Min's house—and Mrs. Kim-Franklin vacuums every afternoon at three o'clock. Of course, Annabelle tended to be pretty dirty and covered in food. That's because she's a pig.

Annabelle had a habit of rummaging through neighbors' gardens. In fact, on the day that *The Cub Report* became a real newspaper, with issues given to everyone in Bear Creek, all police were called to the scene of a break-in . . . which ended up being Annabelle pushing through the front door of a neighbor's house to get to a freshly baked pie.

"No one's going to take *The Cub Report* seriously if our top-of-the-fold story is a pig pie theft."

"But we don't fold our newspaper. We roll it." Min was still waving her twenty-dollar bill.

I sighed again.

"The Wrinkler family was at the diner last night," Gloria said. "They told me Annabelle helped herself to their garden carrots last night. And then the Thompsonses said she ate all their lettuce. But the Thompsonses aren't all that reliable. When they went to pay their bill, Mr. Thompsons couldn't find his wallet and Mrs. Thompsons forgot her purse, so Dad had to put their meal on a tab. Again."

"All right," I said. "We've got to follow the news, even if it's boring. Thom, how about you cover the Annabelle story? Remember, keep it to the big five."

Every news story had to cover *who, what, where, when,* and *why.*

Thom nodded and walked toward the barn doors.

"Where are you going?" I asked.

"To interview Annabelle," he said.

"You can't interview Annabelle."

"Why not?" Thom asked.

"Well, for starters, because she's a pig. Besides, you don't even have a notebook!" I always have a reporter's notebook and two pens in my back pocket. Thom's cut-off jean shorts had a huge hole in the back pocket. I handed him a notebook from my backpack and a blue and a red pen. He tucked a pen behind each ear, pulling back the sides of his shaggy blond hair, and headed out.

Thom's different from anyone I have ever met. I was pretty sure he would've interviewed a pig. He was a careful writer and he noticed things a lot of people overlooked. I'd make a journalist out of him yet.

Gordon pushed off the side of the barn. He kicked on the edge of his skateboard, popping it up so he could grab it with his outstretched hand. With the other, he shifted the camera hanging around his neck. "I'll catch up to Thom—maybe get a shot of Annabelle in action."

I looked down at the budget list. So far, it had only Annabelle on it.

My heart hammered as I thought about the *Bear Creek Gazette,* the town newspaper that had closed for good earlier this month. Now *The Cub Report* was the only independent press in town; if we couldn't make this newspaper work, no one would have access to local news.

"Did you hear what happened in Burlington Meadows?" Gloria asked.

Burlington Meadows was a town about two hours south of us. Mom and I had spent the night there when we moved from the city. I remember thinking it was a teeny tiny town, only to discover it is twice the size of Bear Creek. But surely even exciting things happen in teeny tiny towns, right? Things other than pie-stealing pigs?

"What happened?" Min asked, bouncing on her toes. She had a tendency to bounce. Sometimes she even skipped. Despite this, she was a good friend, even if she did argue with me way more than necessary.

"Well, you know how there's a prison in Windham?"

"Yes!" Min and I said at the same time, though I was pretty sure neither of us knew that.

Gloria leaned forward, her elbow on her knee. Her eyebrows peaked and her mouth twitched. Gloria always knew everything going on in town, thanks to the diner, and she loved dishing it out. Her writing would benefit from fewer exclamation points, though; I could even hear them when she talked, too. "Well, some prisoners were being transferred to another location, right? And the van stopped in Burlington Meadows for gas. Somehow a prisoner *escaped*! He's been loose ever since! There are, like, a million police officers in Burlington Meadows. They even have hound dogs searching for the guy's scent!"

"Wow," Charlotte whispered.

The four of us looked at each other, all thinking the same thing: *Why couldn't anything like that happen here in Bear Creek?*

An escaped prisoner? That was a top-of-the-fold news story for sure.

There's never a shortage of news, just a lack of insight. This was one of my dad's favorite sayings. He'd tell it to any reporter who complained about not having a story. *Go out and find one. Everyone has a story.*

"Everyone has a story," I said aloud. "There are lots of interesting stories right here in Bear Creek, I'm sure. We just have to leave the newsroom, meet people, and scout out their stories."

"I'm not allowed to talk to strangers," Min said. She waved her money again. "I *am* allowed to get ice cream."

Gloria tilted her head toward Min and nodded. "Same."

"Min, it's not talking with strangers if you're a reporter. It's literally the job," I said.

"It's literally going to get me in trouble," Min said and crossed her arms. She looked a lot like her mom when she did that.

Gloria fanned herself with the back of her hand and blew air up on her bangs again. "As someone who works with the Bear Creek public on the regular, I can tell you that some people's stories are that they're boring and need to get a life. Kind of like we need to get ice cream."

I stood and put my hands on my hips. "I could go anywhere in Bear Creek, meet anyone, and have a story by tonight. It's all in the questions."

"Prove it," Charlotte suddenly said. She strolled over to the map of Bear Creek on the barn wall and studied it for a second. "If everyone has a story, like you say, go here"—she pointed to an intersection at the far western edge of Bear Creek—"and find the person who lives there. Get their story."

Quiet Charlotte suddenly looked fierce. "Prove it," she said again.

CHAPTER TWO

WHEN I LIVED IN the city, I had my own subway pass. And that was when I was only ten.

Now I'm nearly twelve and live in a town whose whole population is less than my previous school district's, but when Charlotte pointed to a random intersection on the west side of town, I wasn't exactly sure it'd be okay for me to go there by myself.

In the city, I never felt alone because there were moms and dads pushing strollers, shops with Open signs in the windows, and police officers on nearly every block. Bear Creek had actual *bears*. It also had long stretches of lonely woods where there was no cell phone reception.

I reminded myself that I was named after Nellie Bly, the founder of investigative journalism. *That* Nellie traveled the whole world by herself; she wouldn't be nervous about going a couple miles outside of town. Not that I was scared. However, today did seem like a nice day for a walk with a friend. "So, who's coming with me?" I asked the Cubs.

"Sorry." Min tucked her allowance into her mouse bag. "I have plans."

"Me, too," Gloria said.

Charlotte, her cheeks still pink from speaking so loudly, lowered her head.

"Do your plans happen to be getting ice cream?" I asked.

Min smiled.

I straightened my back. "Okay. I'll do the *lead* feature this issue. And you guys maybe won't even have an article. That's *fine*."

Gloria turned to Min. "I heard Miss Juliet added a new flavor—Bittersweet Mint—at the creamery. I think that's what I'm going to get."

I growled. Neither Min nor Gloria looked my way. Charlotte continued to study her dirty canvas sneakers. "Charlotte?"

She shook her head. "I think I have some copy editing to do."

"We don't have any stories yet. How could you edit stories that haven't been written?"

Charlotte's birdlike shoulders peaked and fell.

"Fine." I paused to study the map.

"Corner of Appleyard and Morgan Roads," Charlotte whispered.

"I know." I snapped a picture of the map with my cell phone. I marched toward the barn doors, but slowly, in case any of them felt the immense guilt that should've accompanied calling out their editor and then leaving her to write a story on her own. The three continued discussing Bittersweet Mint.

Know what I love? Mint ice cream.

Everyone has a story, I heard in Dad's voice. With a heavy sigh that no one seemed to notice, I trudged across the street to my house so I could tell Mom I was heading out for a story.

This is what my life had come to: skipping ice cream *and* checking in with my mom. The price for quality journalism in a small town is high.

————————————————

Mom wasn't home.

Fact: Mom was *always* home.

Since we had moved from the city, she spent all day every day in the attic. Not because she had turned into a bat or anything; she was working on a book, or at least that was what she told me. I was pretty sure she was working on not missing Dad so much.

My dad had been an incredible journalist. I know how to be the *Cub Report* news editor because he had been the news editor of a major newspaper. People listened to Dad. Not because he was loud—he almost never raised his voice (except when someone forgot to fill the coffeepot). People cared what he had to say because he was smart and he was careful, especially with other people's stories. That made him important.

I wanted to be like that. I *was* going to be like that, starting with this story, the one I was going to scout out in the middle of Nowhere, Bear Creek.

I texted Mom. *Hey, where are you?*

The three dots danced on my screen instantly. *I'm at the creamery getting coffee with Juliet. All ok?*

For a moment, everything turned black. What kind of Bittersweet Mint misery was this? Everyone getting ice cream but me? I growled so loudly the sound echoed in the empty attic. Something scurried in a corner. I tried not to think about what it could be.

Fine. I texted back. I took a deep breath. *Tell Miss Juliet I say hi.* It was a good thing Mom and Miss Juliet were hanging out. *The Cub Report* kind of brought them together, I guess. Our first issue had profiled the ice cream maker. Thom's reporting shared that Miss Juliet's mother had died a few years earlier. So, she and Mom had something in common; both were mourning. Something squished in my heart. I missed Dad so much that I didn't have words for it. (And as the daughter of two journalists, I always had words.)

Sometimes I let myself believe Dad was simply on a long business trip to Asia. But I had stopped telling other people that—it seemed to make them really worried. It's just the story I told myself sometimes.

I straightened my back and sent another text to Mom. *Going to interview someone for the paper. Corner of Morgan and Appleyard Roads. Okay?* Mom must've been enjoying her ice cream because I didn't see the three dots. I tucked the phone into my backpack, then trotted down the steps to the kitchen for a bottle of water. On a hot day like this, cool water was even better than ice cream.

That's a lie.

I slipped the water bottle into my bag, made sure I had my notebook and two pens, then hopped on my bike and headed toward Morgan Road.

Dad would be excited to hear about how I scouted out a story all by myself.

Appleyard Road was farther away than I thought. A few times, I pulled up the map on my phone just to make sure I was heading in the right direction.

As I pedaled up Morgan Road, the street became narrower. Pine trees on both sides soared toward a clear blue sky. The grass bordering the road was patchy and tall. Birds chirped all around and squirrels darted in front of me like they had never seen a bicycle before. A few cars and pickup trucks passed, but the farther I pedaled, the fewer signs of human life I saw. The way was almost entirely uphill. I tried not to think about how I was going to have to go down the hill to get home. Fact: I'd always pick going uphill over downhill.

Gravity was so bossy.

Some people (ahem, Min) say that *I'm* bossy. That's not true. I'm reliably right and thoughtful in my approach.

Finally, I saw the Appleyard Road sign. I stepped off the bike and stood at the intersection, looking around. If I was going to tell someone's story from this part of town, I was going to have to find a person, and *that* was going to be tricky, given there was only one house in sight. And that house looked, well, kind of scary.

I sucked on my bottom lip, considering.

I got out my notebook, flipped to a fresh page, and wrote. *Lots of weeds along very long driveway.* Then I scratched out the word *very*. Once, I had overheard Dad tell a reporter that *very* was a tool for lazy writers. It actually made something weaker to write it. The reporter had written that it was very difficult for someone to get a permit in the city. *If it's difficult, say it's difficult. Saying it's* very *difficult introduces the idea that some things might be* more *difficult,* Dad had told her.

The driveway was long, stretching back and curving slightly so I could just barely make out the house at the end. Again, I turned to my notebook. *Grand-looking house. White, or at least once was white. Now grayish. Two stories with black shutters and a huge wraparound porch.* I squinted down the driveway. *One rocker on the porch.* Though the house was much larger than the little old farmhouse Mom and I lived in, something about it reminded me of home. If I tilted my head when looking at my house, I could see glimmers of how it had looked when new. This house, I bet, once had been glorious.

"Well, are you going to go or not?"

I immediately looked up to the sky. People in Bear Creek had a habit of hanging out in trees. I unsnapped my helmet to make sure I could see. But no one was in the trees around me. Instead, behind me stood a tall, older woman. Quickly, I scribbled in my notebook: *Woman with long white hair. Walking stick. Angry voice.*

"Are you writing about me, young lady?" the woman asked.

"No," I blurted. "I mean, yes." I slipped the pen into the ring of the notebook and thrust out my hand to shake hers. Her hand was strong and callused, and it surprised me. I guess I was expecting soft, tissue-thin skin like my grandma's. "I'm Nellie Murrow, news editor of *The Cub Report.*"

The woman's eyebrows mushed together and so did her lips. "*The Cub Report?*"

"It's a real newspaper."

"Is that right?" the woman replied. "I'm Patricia Wilkonson. A reporter, huh? Well, then, I assume you're here to talk to me about my pen. I wondered if I'd hear from the media today."

"Your what?" I snagged my own pen back out of my notebook.

"My pen. The one used by the governor twenty years ago today. I still have it, 'course. I'll show it to you for your *real* newspaper."

I really wished she hadn't used air quotes when she said *real*.

"Follow me."

———————————————

I paused on Ms. Wilkonson's porch. "I'll wait out here."

She tilted her head at me and nodded. "I like smarts in a kid. Don't go in strangers' houses." She wagged a finger at me. "You shouldn't be here alone, either."

"You sound like my grandma," I said.

Ms. Wilkonson's face flared a deep red, and she disappeared into her house. Soon she came back cradling a small glass box that contained a black velvet cushion. On that cushion was a pen. I leaned in to look closer. Yep, just a pen. Other towns had escaped prisoners. My town had a pen. A blue pen with a golden seal featuring a pine tree with two old-fashioned men on either side. One had an anchor resting on his shin. The other held a sickle.

"That's the governor's seal," said Ms. Wilkonson, her chin pitched high.

"Uh-huh," I said. The screen door was slow to close, so I had a peek at the interior of her house. Though the pen had its own special display case, the rest of the house looked a lot like the dining room in my house—which is where Mom and I piled everything we hadn't unpacked since our move. It seemed like Ms. Wilkonson didn't know where to put anything other than the pen in its special case right inside the front door.

I got that finger-twirling feeling when a story starts whispering for me to take some notes. I flipped my notebook to a fresh page and wondered how best to phrase my first question. Dad always said reporters' questions should be specific and, whenever possible, should require something more than a yes or no answer. I peeked into the house through the screen. "So, why do you take such great care of your pen, but your house looks like Annabelle the Pig went on a rampage inside?"

Only at that moment I must've stepped right into a cell reception opening because before Ms. Wilkonson could answer, my phone erupted. *Ping! Ping! Ping!* Texts from Mom, Gloria, Min, Gordon, and even Thom, who hated to use his phone. Mostly Mom, though. And then the steady *burr* of an incoming call. Without waiting for Ms. Wilkonson to answer my question, I answered the phone.

Mom, her voice high and scared, said, "Nellie? Are you okay? Tell me you're okay!"

"I'm fine, Mom!"

Mom's exhale seemed to go right through the phone to inflate my own suddenly shaky lungs. "Nellie!" she yelped. "Where are you? Do you have any idea what just happened in Bear Creek?"

CHAPTER THREE

MOM WASN'T ABLE TO give me much information; she had been trying too hard to reach me to scout out the details. If that doesn't show you how much Bear Creek had changed her, nothing would. She was a crime reporter in the city! All she knew was there had been a crime or accident downtown and police were swarming the scene. In the background, I heard sirens. "The roads are blocked, so I can't come get you. I need you to get back here, Nellie," Mom said before we hung up.

"I have to go," I said to Ms. Wilkonson and then scribbled my name and number on a blank piece of paper and thrust it at her. "Breaking news in Bear Creek!"

"This *is* Bear Creek," Ms. Wilkonson said. "The outer edge of it, but still—"

"Thanks! Bye!" I ran off the porch and down the driveway. Quick as I could, I snapped my helmet onto my head and mounted the bike.

Behind me, Ms. Wilkonson called from her porch: "But what about my pen?"

"Yes, it's really cool," I lied over my shoulder.

I didn't even consider the fact that I'd be going downhill as I jumped onto the bike, steering one-handed so I could hold my phone and listen to my voicemail message from Thom. "Nellie, we're at the scene. Don't worry, I found some paper. Gordon's really the one covering things, though. You know, the who, where, and whatnot. Where are you?"

Who, where, and whatnot? *Whatnot?* No, Thom! No!

I pedaled faster down the hill.

But since I also was holding my phone in front of me, trying to read the texts (which included an all-caps one from Min: *WHERE ARE YOU, NELLIE MURROW? NINER NINER STUFF IS HAPPENING! OVER OUT!*), gravity got bossy. The front handles of my bike jerked back and forth. I held on to the right-hand grip with my fingers also wrapped around my phone. Then the handlebars seemed to vibrate all over.

The wheels swirled, shooting up pieces of gravel into my legs. I missed the pedal, and it slammed me in the shin. Next thing I knew, I was sprawled out in the tall grass.

I kicked one leg. Then the other. They stung a little and they were pretty scratched up, but they worked. Next, I lifted my arms. Both functional. Still sprawled on my back, I unsnapped my helmet, lifting it off of my head. Then I twisted my neck back and forth. Yep, still moved.

I pushed up to my feet. I smooshed the helmet back onto my head, even though I felt the crunch of briar clusters against my scalp. I'd deal with them later. For now, I had a story to cover.

Sirens in Bear Creek! I entered downtown with my feet still slipping off the pedals and my shins taking the brunt of the pedals' force, not that I noticed. Breaking news! In Bear Creek!

Police cars streaked by me, many of them from neighboring towns. Whatever was going on was *big*!

I followed the line of police cars to the scene. Swerving past parked squad cars and ambulances, I soon reached a line of yellow caution tape. There, I finally stepped off the bike, letting it drop into the grass by the curb.

Annabelle the Pig's house was the scene of the crime.

For a moment—just a brief, not-even-real nanosecond—something boiled inside me. *I was admiring a* pen *while Thom and Gordon covered the biggest story* ever *in Bear Creek?* Then I reminded myself not to make assumptions; maybe this was some sort of drill—so I grabbed for my notebook and pens that were in my back pocket.

Empty. My pocket was empty.

A reporter without a notebook or a pen? Gah! It was worse than missing a scoop!

A few steps from the cluster of police officers, I realized I was still wearing my bicycle helmet. Quickly, I unsnapped it and tossed it back to where my bike was sprawled. Thankfully, the police were on the open side of the caution tape. Crossing into a crime scene would have hefty consequences for both the journalist, who could face police charges, and the police officers, whose investigation could be compromised.

I pushed my hands through my hair, trying to smooth it before I approached the officers. I felt bunches of bumps and snags from the briars. No time to deal with that now. The press couldn't wait for combed hair!

"Excuse me." I stood behind the officers, all of whom were talking at once.

They ignored me.

"Excuse me!" I said louder. Sometimes journalists must fight to be heard, but they have every right to ask questions. The First Amendment guaranteed it!

One of the officers glanced my way and then back to the notebook in his hand. Then it was like his face had gotten snagged on a briar in my hair. His gaze snapped back to me. His mouth popped open. The officer, who must've been from a neighboring town because I didn't recognize him, jerked his hand out to the officer next to him. She glanced at the first officer's face, then followed his eyes to me. Like him, her mouth popped open. But she closed hers, her shoulders shaking silently like she was suppressing a cough. That got the attention of the other officers, all of whom turned to face me. Finally, some respect for the press.

"Yes," I said in my serious-reporter voice (think regular voice mixed with a little grout). "Nellie Murrow of *The Cub Report*. A few questions. First, does anyone have a notebook I can borrow?"

And then one of the officers began to laugh. At me.

"Did you lose in a fight with Annabelle?" He gestured behind him to the pig, where she sat with a big, gummy smile on her face. Annabelle was black and white, about the size of a small wheelbarrow. Her favorite thing to do, aside from stealing vegetables from the neighbors, was to sit in mud with her mouth open in a big, goofy grin. She seemed to be laughing at me, too.

Soon all of the police officers were chuckling except for one—Bear Creek Police Department Chief Rodgers. He sighed, his barrel chest rising and falling as exhaled hot air made the edges of his too-long mustache twitch. "We already gave interviews to *The Cub Report*."

"But I just got here."

"Check with your star reporter." Again, the chief's mustache twitched.

"*I'm* the—"

"Nellie?" Breaking through the cluster of officers and coming from *inside* the yellow tape, Gordon strode toward me. His camera swung from his neck. He paused. "What happened to you?"

"What are you talking about?" I straightened my back. "I'm here to report!"

He slowly raised the camera and snapped, then handed me the camera. In the little square showing the digital image, I saw myself. My hair was so snagged with briars that it shot out in every direction like porcupine quills. My face was smeared with streaks and scratches. My gray T-shirt was tattered and dirty. My eyes were two wide circles with an open circle mouth. "I look like—"

"A troll doll," Min finished. I turned to see her, perfectly composed in a flurry of ruffles, with Gloria, Charlotte, and Thom.

We Cub reporters huddled next to Annabelle's pen. Thom handed me the notebook and pens I had given him earlier. I flipped open to a clean page. "Okay, we've got to get all of the details down as soon as possible before we forget anything. Tell me exactly what happened, Gordon."

Gordon nodded. His cheeks were shiny and his eyes slightly narrowed. I knew that look. That's the look of someone who has a story about to burst inside him.

"So, me and Thom"—Gordon pointed between the two of them as Charlotte silently mouthed *Thom and I*—"went to interview Annabelle like you said to."

"Actually, I said Annabelle was a pig and . . ."

Gordon raised an eyebrow. I gestured for him to continue. "Anyway, when we got here, Thom went to the front to talk to the human Murphys."

"Good decision." I flashed Thom a thumbs-up. He grinned.

Gordon continued, "And I went to the side yard to photograph Annabelle. She was out of her pigpen, sitting in the mud and smiling, you know how she does?" We all nodded, except for Min, who instead reenacted the pig's superwide smile.

"I know from talking with the Murphys—I mow their lawn once in a while—that Annabelle does smile because when she was a piglet, Mrs. Murphy would give her a treat for smiling."

Something pulled at my hair. I looked over my shoulder to see Gloria's scrunched-up face. She was tugging at one of the briars. "You might have to shave your head," she said. "I don't know how those briars are going to come out of it."

"I'll worry about that later. We have to focus," I said and stepped away from her.

"Hey!" Min rubbed her cheek. "You hit me with your thorny stick head."

"I don't have a stick head," I snapped.

"You're the one who's always saying we have to be precise. Your head is *precisely* full of thorny sticks." Min pushed my shoulder so I wasn't standing within prickly distance of her. "Scarecrow," she muttered.

I ignored her.

Gordon took a breath and continued: "Annabelle was facing the pigpen, which I thought was pretty weird. Because she only smiles at people. But if she was out of the pigpen and Thom was interviewing Mr. and Mrs. Murphy, who was in the pigpen? I lifted my camera to see if I could zoom in and figure out what was going on inside the pen. The next thing I knew, I saw a leg!"

"A leg?" we all echoed.

"Yeah, a human leg. It was hanging from the pigpen window. And then the leg went back inside. A couple seconds later, out popped a head."

"A head?" we echoed again.

"Are you guys going to keep doing that? Because it's pretty annoying."

We all closed our mouths. Gordon nodded. "Good. Okay, so a head popped out and then a torso. This person was trying to squeeze through the pigpen window. Since the window's on the side of the pigpen and not visible from inside the house, I guessed the guy was trying to escape. He was wearing a jumpsuit. One of the orange ones, even though just about every inch of it was coated in mud. Sort of like you right now, Nellie. But I'm pretty sure he *tried* to cover himself up in mud."

He didn't say it mean—just like a fact. But the comparison wasn't necessary.

Gordon rubbed the back of his neck as I rearranged my face out of a scowl. "Anyway," he said, "the guy's clothes were super bulky. Through the lens, I could see that was because the jumpsuit was stuffed with vegetables—zucchini and apples—like he had just shoved the food down the front. I kept my lens on him and somehow managed to snap a bunch of pics while also pressing down the call button Nellie made us all create on our phones so we could contact Chief Rodgers super quickly. I knew by then that this was the guy—the escaped prisoner from Burlington Meadows!"

I punched Gordon's shoulder, so proud I could've hugged him right then and there, but I remembered two important things: one—my hair probably would've impaled him; and two—I'm not a hugger.

"Weren't you scared?" Min held her hands to her face. "I mean, he's an escaped prisoner! And he was right in front of you!"

Gordon shrugged, but he tucked his tongue into his cheek like he was trying not to grin.

"Yeah, I guess if I had thought about it. But I was so focused. I knew this was a big story."

I must've squealed or something because Gordon took a step back from me.

"Besides," he said, "I knew he wasn't going to make it out of the window, even if he *did* see me. He was so super bulky he couldn't fit. Not just with, you know, vegetables. It looked like he had loaves of bread and containers of other stuff hidden under his clothes. Sure enough, he got stuck, right in the window. Like upside down, hanging from his waist. I saw all this jewelry and a couple wallets trickle off of him, too."

Min snorted, which set Thom into a giggle fit. Gordon gave a sideways grin. "I just started snapping all of these pics." He flipped backward through the shots on his camera. "Soon, I had Chief Rodgers on the phone. I told him he better hurry over to the Murphys. Less than three minutes later, Chief was here. That's when I got these shots."

Gordon turned the camera toward the group of us and we gathered around, Thom standing close to me even though the briars must've pricked his cheek.

"There!" I called as he showed us the images. On the screen was the prisoner, wedged in the window, face twisted and arms awkwardly raised toward Chief Rodgers, who held his stun gun pointed toward him. In the background Annabelle sat and smiled at them both. *"That's* our top of the fold, Cubs!"

Thom, Min, Gloria, Charlotte, and I clapped Gordon on the back and cheered.

"All right, guys." I raised my hands to quiet the crew. "We have a special issue to produce!"

CHAPTER FOUR

CHIEF RODGERS SIGHED AS I strode toward him with my notebook in hand. I pushed at sprigs of spiky hair, tucking them into the baseball cap Charlotte let me borrow before she headed back to her house to gather information on the Burlington Meadows prison.

The Cub reporters had quickly divvied up the potential stories, each of us taking a different angle. I was going to cover the **press conference** Chief Rodgers was holding at the police station. When there is a major break in a case or a big crime-related news story, police often host a press conference to make sure the media get the facts at the same time and to give reporters a chance to ask questions all at once rather than tying up the officers with lots of individual interviews.

Gordon came with me to get pictures of the chief as he explained the details of the prisoner's capture. Thom was going to follow up with the Murphys for their reaction to finding a convict in their pigpen. "I'll check in with Annabelle, too," he said. I let that slide.

Min was going to create a timeline of the prisoner's escape. And Gloria was heading to the diner to get reactions from the locals.

All of us were going to meet back at the barn in an hour to compile our stories.

"There are a lot of real reporters here," Gordon whispered at the press conference. Adults hoisting huge news cameras on their shoulders volleyed for space among a half dozen reporters from regional newspapers and news stations, who crowded around the podium.

"*We're* real reporters." I straightened my back. He did, too. "And we were first on the scene. None of these guys got the shots you got, Gordon."

He nodded, tucking his tongue into his cheek again, and held up his camera at the ready.

"Hey, kid." Both Gordon and I turned around, but the reporter was focused on Gordon. He held a notebook in his hand and wore a button-down shirt and khakis. He smirked and I didn't like the way his lip curled. "Randolph Yellow of the *Burlington Meadows Journal.* I heard you got a picture of the escapee."

Gordon smiled back. "Yes, sir."

The man held out his hand for Gordon's camera. "Give me the flash drive and I'll upload it to my laptop." He shifted so Gordon could see the canvas backpack he was wearing.

"Uhh . . ." Gordon's eyes cut toward me.

I stepped forward. "Nellie Murrow," I said, extending my hand toward him, "news editor of *The Cub Report.* Gordon's images will be in our special issue tomorrow."

His eyebrow popped. So maybe the hat wasn't covering *all* the briars. And maybe my face was still smeared with dirt. And, yeah, there were scratches up my arms and legs. But I *was* a news editor. *"Or,"* Randolph said, drawing out the word like it had sixteen *R*s, "it could run in the *Burlington Meadows Journal."*

"No," I said. *"We* got the scoop and we'll be running the picture."

"Shouldn't you be playing in a sandbox somewhere?" Randolph Yellow snickered.

I squeezed my hand into a fist. "Shouldn't *you* be doing your own reporting instead of stealing it from so-called kids?"

"I'm talking to the photographer now. Run along." He waved me away and turned to Gordon, saying, "I'll give you credit in the caption, kid, if it means that much to you."

I pressed my lips together, stifling the rage rising in my body.

Randolph Yellow laughed, a huffy, coughy sound. "Cool it, kiddo," he said to me. "It's just a picture."

That's when my fist reminded me about the years of martial arts training it had acquired back in the city. Just as I was about to lurch forward, a hand pressed on my shoulder. I heard another sigh. Chief Rodgers.

The reporter turned back to Gordon. "Your choice. Be published in a big paper or not." He held out his hand.

Gordon rubbed the back of his neck, then looked at the reporter. "I'm on assignment now. For my newspaper. Maybe the *Burlington Meadows Journal* can send its photographer over to the pigpen. I bet Annabelle will smile for him. She smiles for anyone."

Chief Rodgers whispered, "Atta boy." But when I looked up he simply cleared his throat and took to the stage. "All right, folks," he spoke into the microphone, then launched into the facts of the case. "Windham Prison inmate Charles MacDew, who escaped in Burlington Meadows during a prison transfer, was apprehended this afternoon by myself, Police Chief Henry Rodgers, as he attempted to flee the scene of a robbery in Bear Creek. He appears to have been hiding in an outside structure alongside a farm animal. Upon seeing two juveniles approaching the home, MacDew attempted to flee with stolen property. He is now back in custody and awaiting trial for the new charges, including larceny, burglary, trespassing, and more."

I scribbled into my notebook. Then Chief paused. His mustache twitched, which I knew was a sign that he was irritated. He crossed his hands over his big barrel belly. "I'll take questions now."

I raised my hand in the air, even though it barely reached the shoulders of some of the other reporters. All around me, people shouted questions. Cameras clicked furiously and video journalists jockeyed for position. Randolph Yellow's voice boomed over my head. I went up on tiptoes, but it felt useless. How could anyone see me? "Over here!" Randolph Yellow said.

To another reporter, he said, "Bet the chief doesn't know how to act—a real crime interrupting a day of eating donuts in this hick town."

Chief Rodgers's eyes narrowed. Scanning the reporters, he said, "Nellie Murrow. You go first."

"*Yes!*" I shouted and bounced like baby Min. All of the reporters silenced around me, searching, I guessed, for the new reporter.

Randolph Yellow groaned. "The kid?"

"Go ahead, Nellie," the chief said, even though his eyes were narrowed on the older journalist. "Ask your question."

"*Questions,* Chief. I've got a few. First: How long do you believe the suspect was hiding in Bear Creek?"

———————————

I stopped quickly at home to grab the laptop Mom let me use. We had been texting while I was at the scene, so she knew I was safe. I had even texted that I fell off my bike and had a couple scrapes. Still, I suppose I should've warned her about how I looked.

"Nellie! Your hair!" she said rather loudly.

"It's fine, Mom," I said. "We'll deal with it after the paper is out."

"*We'll deal with it after the paper is out?*" Mom echoed. "You are such your father's daughter."

"Thank you," I called as I shut the front door behind me.

An hour later, in the newsroom, Stuff pulled briars out of my hair with his buck teeth.

"Not now, Stuff." I pushed the goat away without looking up from my laptop. "I'm on deadline!" The goat brayed at me but trotted over to nibble on Thom's shoe instead.

Gloria's piece on the local reaction looked really great as a tower of stand-alone **pull quotes,** or direct statements, next to the huge picture of the prisoner dangling from Annabelle's pen. The headline across the top read: *Escaped prisoner back in the pen!*

"I don't get it," Min said as she read over my shoulder. "He got out of the pigpen."

"It's a play on words," I said. "Like how the pen is what they call the penitentiary or prison. And Annabelle lives in a pigpen."

Min blinked at me. "Sometimes I think you're older than my dad. And he's really old."

"I'm eleven," I snapped.

"If you didn't play with dolls, I wouldn't believe it."

"Those aren't *dolls*. They're—"

"*Story devices*," chanted the entire newsroom.

I ignored them and went back to scanning the **mock-up** of the paper. On one row beside the huge picture was my news story with the facts of the case. The first paragraph was the most important:

```
Windham Prison escapee, Charles MacDew, 42,
is back in police custody tonight follow-
ing his capture in a Bear Creek pigpen,
where police suspect the convicted burglar
had been hiding for several days, shar-
ing space with Annabelle the Pig, whom
neighbors blamed for their missing produce,
jewelry and pie.
```

The rest of the article detailed how MacDew had spotted a reporter at the Murphys' front door and tried to escape from the pigpen window with his stolen food and jewelry.

"Why can't we say Thom's name here instead of 'a *Cub Report* reporter'?" Charlotte asked. She also was reading the copy over my shoulder.

When my dad was in journalism school, he had an internship at a small city newspaper. He told me one of his first articles was about an elderly couple whose front yard constantly flooded after rainstorms because of ineffective irrigation at the new city park. So, he had waited until it rained, then went to the couple's house. The elderly man waved him to park his car in the grass beside the driveway. As soon as he stepped out, Dad's foot sunk up to his ankle in mud. "Now you're good and stuck, like us," the old man had said. Dad had to call a tow company to pull his mud-dredged car out of the soaked yard. He had wanted to include that tidbit in the article, but his news editor changed it to "a visitor's car" that had to be towed. *I learned an important lesson that day, Nellie,* Dad told me when he shared this story. *The only place my name belonged in the paper was on the byline.*

"Why?" I had asked Dad.

"Because it's our job as journalists to report the news, not to *be* the news," I said to Charlotte now, giving her the same reply Dad had given me.

Thom was sitting on a hay bale next to Stuff, also reviewing the mock-up with his phone and a clipboard. As exciting as it was to have a special edition, pushing through a whole issue in a couple hours meant every one of us had to **fact-check** each other's work and look for mistakes.

Min had made a form to make checking facts easier for everyone—at the top was printed *Fact Check Sheet*. Under it was a column for us to list all proper names, addresses, or phone numbers used in an article. Beside that were three more columns for us to make note of how we had checked, double-checked, and triple-checked that the information was accurate. To make sure we had spelled Charles MacDew correctly, Thom noted in the Check One column that he had compared the spelling to that used in the press release from Bear Creek Police Department. The second check was a previous news article in the *Burlington Meadows Journal* about when MacDew had been convicted. The third check was a listing online for his former address.

"Can you believe this?" Thom said.

"What?" I asked. "Do you see a mistake?"

"No," Thom laughed. "I was just thinking about how this morning we couldn't think of anything to fill the next newspaper, and now here we are, finishing one in record time."

———————————

"I'm telling you, this will be better than wasting time on a website," Gloria said. "At the diner, I see what everyone's doing. They're not on the *New York Times*'s website. They're liking—and sharing—social media posts."

"But none of us are old enough to have social media accounts," Min pointed out.

"It's not like social media companies check our IDs," Gloria said. "We could create one account and just *say* that we're old enough."

"*No,*" Min and I said at the same time. (Min because she's a natural rule follower, me because, as news editor, I *had* to follow the rules.)

"What if we had permission?" Charlotte suggested. "We could ask our parents."

"*No!*" This time the response came from me and Gordon.

"If we're going to truly be an independent press, we shouldn't have to get permission from anyone other than a Cub reporter or editor to handle a story," I said. We all turned to Gordon, thinking he'd also share why he thought that was a bad idea, but he just rubbed the back of his neck.

I had noticed when working on our last issue that Gordon wasn't super close with his mom. Dr. Burke ran the school district; I thought she'd be proud of Gordon since he was so smart and kind and artistic and incredibly handsome and . . .

Back to my point—she didn't seem to see all that when she looked at Gordon. Instead, she was always suggesting different things Gordon could be doing with his time. Of course, maybe that's because he hid a lot from her. When we were researching crow behavior at the local university a few weeks earlier, Gordon hadn't told his mom that he usually sat in on photography classes; he told her instead that he skateboarded around the campus.

"What if we made it easier for people to post our stories to their accounts?" Charlotte said in her half-whispery way. She grabbed the laptop and typed in the *Burlington Meadows Journal* address. "See? All of the articles here have a little button at the bottom that lets people post to social media sites automatically."

"Min, do you know how to do that?" I asked.

Min rolled her eyes. "Of course I don't. I'm not allowed on social media. But I bet my dad could show me. He helped set up our website, after all."

About an hour later, Min texted us that her dad had added the social media option to our website articles. I went over to her house to print the second-ever issue of *The Cub Report*. They were still warm when the other Cub reporters gathered on Min's porch for delivery.

"Ready?" I divvied up the issues into piles. The rest of the news staff stood around me on Min's porch, bicycles, skateboards, and scooters at the ready. "Same delivery routes as last time and same teams—Min and Charlotte, Gordon and Gloria, Thom and me. We'll meet up at Wells Diner in forty minutes."

"Are you sure you don't want to . . ." Gloria pointed vaguely at my head.

"Oh," I said, remembering the briar patch.

Thom grinned. "I've got this. You can . . ." He also gestured toward my hair.

Off they went, sharing breaking news with Bear Creek neighbors. I walked across the Kim-Franklins' lush grass to our house's brittle lawn to deal with my briar-filled head.

Little did I know that reception for this issue of *The Cub Report* would be just as thorny.

CHAPTER FIVE

"WHAT ARE WE GOING to do?" Mom sat in front of me with a comb, a tub of mayonnaise, and a bowl of ice. This was the tenth time she asked the question.

Mom had found an online article that claimed mayonnaise sometimes made hair slippery enough for briars to slide out. She also read that ice could make it easier to get gum out of hair, and because the mayonnaise wasn't working, she had tried ice. Now I had frozen globs of mayonnaise *and* briars stuck to my head. "I think it's time for scissors," she said.

"No!" I yelped. I don't really *care* about appearances. I wear the same color scheme—black or gray—every day. I comb my hair but keep it in a nice sensible bob. I don't wear makeup. But I also didn't want to be bald.

"You know," Mom said, "when Nellie Bly was willingly committed to the asylum to report on the atrocities there, her head was shaved."

"Is that true?"

"I'm not sure," Mom said. "I just don't know what to do for this mess." She tugged at a bunch of my hair.

I grabbed the comb and started pulling it through my hair.

In the end we had to cut only a few chunks of hair, and luckily they were in the back of my head.

"Are you sure you don't want to go to a stylist and get this cut cleaned up a bit?" Mom asked when I came downstairs after scrubbing the remaining twigs and mayonnaise from my hair. The mayo might not have made my hair briar-free, but it had added a nice glossy glow.

"Nah, it's fine. I have to go meet up with the rest of the club at the diner now."

Mom grabbed her car keys. "I'll give you a lift so you can fill me in on all of the incredible articles I just read on *The Cub Report* website. I'll treat the staff to pizza for dinner, too."

I grinned.

Fact: The Murrow family always celebrated breaking news with pizza.

Mom called Chef Wells from the car to reserve a table and to order three large pizzas and pitchers of soda. When we arrived, the whole club was at the big round table in the middle of the diner. Chef Wells headed down the wheelchair ramp, balancing one of the pizzas on a tray on his lap. When Gloria hopped up to take an order from someone at the register, he waved her back to her seat. "Let Frank and me handle the register today. Celebrate hard work with your friends."

The whole diner was buzzing—almost every one of the mismatched tables was full of Bear Creek residents, regional police officers, and reporters. A happy shiver went up my spine when I spotted copies of *The Cub Report* at most tables.

"Check this out," said Gordon, turning toward me. "Our photo's being picked up by national news!" Sure enough, there was Gordon's photograph on a major news network website. I grabbed his phone to read: *Photo by Gordon Burke / The Cub Report, Bear Creek, Maine.*

The Cub Report was mentioned on national news! "We're a real newspaper," I gasped.

"Of course we're a real newspaper!" Min pushed my shoulder. She leaned in and whispered, "Don't worry about your hair. It'll grow."

All night, Bear Creek residents came to our table to hear Gordon recount his catching the burglar, to laugh about Annabelle's toothy smile, and to congratulate us for breaking the news.

"You're a real hero," Miss Juliet said to Gordon. "Free ice cream all week for Cub reporters."

"Yay!" Min cheered at the same time I said, "No, thank you."

Both Min and Miss Juliet looked at me with confusion on their faces.

"A free and independent press cannot accept free gifts. It would go against our **ethics**," I said.

"Even if we promise to just order vanilla?" Min whined.

"Even then, Min."

———————————

I was totally fine with the fact that Gordon not only got the shot of a lifetime but also broke the case of the missing prisoner. This was such good news. So great. Amazing. So happy for Gordon.

It was absolutely no big deal—at all—that *I* wasn't credited even though my story was right next to Gordon's photograph and *I* was the one who assigned him the story. Of course, that was no big deal. Because, wow! *The Cub Report* was getting so much attention. This was fantastic. Fan-tas-tic.

I kept reminding myself of these facts when the staff met in the newsroom two days after the special edition published.

"I got an email from *Ellen*! For real," Gordon said to the rest of the club. "I mean, she asked if it was okay if they post the pic on their Facebook page. It wasn't Ellen herself, but it was a member of her team." Gordon tucked his tongue into his cheek when Gloria whistled low.

"That's amazing!"

"So amazing," I echoed.

Thom nudged my side. I peeked up from the laptop, and he raised an eyebrow. "Okay?" he whispered.

"Never better. This is awesome. So awesome."

Thom nodded and shifted a little closer to my side. Fact: I love *Ellen*.

"Can you believe this?" Gordon laughed.

"I cannot," I said. And maybe some of the other writers reared back because they thought my voice was gruff due to something silly—like jealousy—but it wasn't. It was *not*. I was simply using my important editor voice. I cleared my throat. "Okay, folks, so our special edition was a success. But now we need to focus on our next issue. I think we should establish *The Cub Report* as a monthly paper, and that means we need a September issue. School starts in two weeks, and we're all going to have time constraints. It'd be better, I think, to put another issue together now and release it just before school starts."

The other Cubs nodded in agreement.

"Great," I said. "Who has story ideas?"

"Well," Charlotte said softly, "what about that one you were working on? The one about Patricia Wilkonson?"

"Oh." Fact: Patricia Wilkonson had left me three voice-mails asking when I was going to come back to talk about her pen. "I'm still gathering facts."

Gordon's phone buzzed. "Holy smokes! It's CNN! They want to do a profile."

"Of the burglar?" I asked. "They could just read our special edition. We have—"

"No, on *me!*" He read aloud: "'We're intrigued by your newspaper's coverage of the escaped convict in Bear Creek and would like to profile you as an aspiring twelve-year-old journalist.'"

"Aspiring?" I repeated but was drowned out by cheers from the rest of the crew.

"Oh no! I've got to go tell my mom," Gordon said. "They need parental permission."

"Parental permission?" I must've said it super loudly because everyone stopped and blinked at me. I stood up. "Tell them no. The whole point of the Newspaper Club is that it's ours. We don't need parental permission for any of our stories."

Gordon's face twisted a little. "What's your problem, Nellie?"

"Look," I said, "I think it's really incredible that you got that shot for the paper. You were at the right place at the right time—thanks to *me*. But now this whole thing is becoming about you instead of the news. Getting parental permission, talking with *Ellen*? That's not being a journalist. The club is for journalists. Not for nonstop attention over a lucky shot."

The words flew out of my mouth before my head had time to sort them out. This is the opposite of what usually happens to me in groups, when I have to search and search for words to say out loud. Usually, I wish I could just talk the way other kids my age could. Now, looking back at the shocked, angry faces of my news staff, I wished my brain would go back to working the way it normally did. "I don't mean . . ."

I wanted to explain myself better, but that's when my brain decided to return to its normal routine of not providing words to say. How *could* I explain what I had just said? That the attention on *us* made me uncomfortable? That I didn't want CNN or even *Ellen* changing the club, not when it was just getting started? Not when it was the first time I felt like I had friends, had a purpose, had something I made, something that wasn't tied up in everything I had lost?

Without another word to the rest of us, Gordon jumped to his feet and stomped from the barn.

Gloria shook her head. She stood and wiped the hay off her legs. "I've got to get back to the diner."

"Shouldn't we talk about this?" Charlotte whispered.

"Yes," Gloria said, her voice hard. "But I *do* have to go. Dad's been working too late at the diner lately. Tonight, we're having a family dinner."

I don't know why, but my eyes filled with tears. "I just think—"

Gloria waved goodbye over her shoulder. Min sighed and said, "I've got to get home, too." Charlotte shot me a long look as she gathered her books into her backpack. She quietly left.

Now it was just me and Thom. "Do you want to talk about—"

"I only want to talk about the paper, about what we can write about in the next issue."

Thom nodded. "Something will come along."

"All I have is a stupid pen as a lead," I muttered. When Thom's eyebrow popped up, I told him about Ms. Wilkonson and her special pen case.

"I wonder what it signed," Thom said.

"What?"

"The pen—I wonder what it signed. My moms have a friend who keeps a pen like that. It was the one the governor used to make it legal for them to get married to each other." Thom leaned back on a hay bale and crossed his arms behind his head. "They got married the next day."

"Wait," I interrupted him. "Your moms couldn't get married?"

Thom nodded. "Not until the end of 2012. Ma officially adopted me shortly afterward."

"Wow." I couldn't imagine someone saying parents couldn't get married.

Thom pulled a sprig of hay from the bale and popped the end of it in his mouth. He chewed on it for a while, looking a whole lot like Stuff, who did the same thing just behind him. "We went to the friends' house for dinner a few weeks ago, and Mom showed me the pen. It looked pretty simple, just a pen, but it wasn't, because its ink changed a lot of things for families like ours."

From where we perched on the hay bale, I could see stars twinkling in the night sky outside of the barn doors, but maybe they were the strings of yellow lights Thom's moms hung from the house to the barn.

"Thom?" Sheila, his ma, called out from the back door of the house. "Honey, come in soon. We have something we want to talk to you about."

"Okay, Ma!" But Thom didn't stir, just kept lying there on his back.

"Don't you want to go in?" If my mom had said she wanted to talk about something with me like that, I'd be inside in a second flat. That never meant good things. That meant *news*. The only time Dad ever used that line on me was when Alejandro, who lived in the apartment across from ours, falsely claimed I had stolen his kitten. I hadn't, of course. Fluff had crawled inside my knapsack and I simply carried him home. The only time Mom had told me we had something to talk about was when she dropped the whole we're-leaving-the-city-and-moving-to-Bear-Creek bomb on me.

But here was Thom, just staring out at the sky. "Thom, shouldn't you go?"

Thom shrugged. "Whatever it is, I'll find out soon enough."

And this was why I was the reporter in charge of breaking news and Thom would probably always stick with the features beat.

Both of us sat in silence (except for Stuff's loud chewing). Then I said, "That pen, the one you saw, did it have a gold seal on it? With a farmer and a fisherman?"

"Yeah." Thom handed me a piece of hay. I sat cross-legged next to him, both of us chewing on hay.

What had Ms. Wilkonson's pen signed? "You know, I think there might be a story there after all."

"Your dad says everybody has a story."

I liked a lot about Thom, but what I liked most was that he said "says" just then.

"It's probably not going to be as exciting as Gordon's story." Even I heard the jealousy in my voice.

Thom propped up on one elbow as he turned to me. "Maybe not to you. But I bet it will be to Ms. Wilkonson."

I heard Dad's voice: *Everybody has a story, and every story is important.*

CHAPTER SIX

I FILLED THE COFFEE pot with grounds and water for Mom so all she'd have to do is push the button when she woke up. Dad used to make the coffee for them both every morning. Mom barely drank coffee anymore, but when she did, she had this little smile on her face, and I knew she was thinking about Dad.

I had told Mom that I'd be heading out to interview Ms. Wilkonson, whom Mom had called the night before. I felt this was an unnecessary invasion in my journalistic pursuits, but Mom said she had to make sure Ms. Wilkonson was a good person before I met with her alone. (I also had been given a big lecture about heading so far out of town alone and talking with her without confirming with Mom.)

Next to the coffee pot, I placed a note: *Mom, I'm heading out to Ms. Wilkonson's house. Be back by lunchtime.*

I loaded up a water bottle, an extra notebook (just in case), and pens and headed for my bike. I kept it on our front porch. In the city, my dad used his bike to get to work on days when he was running too late to walk. Dad would carry it all the way up to our third-floor apartment and keep it right inside the door. We didn't have a porch then, but we did have a little balcony where Mom grew basil and lavender in small pots. This year, she had planted a whole bunch of herbs in a square patch in our backyard, but she kept forgetting to weed them. I tried once, but I'm pretty sure I pulled out all of the oregano. "Next year I'll be a little more with-it," Mom said the last time we talked about the garden. "Maybe we'll even plant some squash."

I hoped she wouldn't be *that* with it. Squash is rightly named and should be squashed.

Mom kept saying that—about being more "with-it" in the future. I wasn't sure what *it* meant, but I thought it was because she wasn't always entirely *here*. Of course, physically she was here. Aside from that time when she was with Miss Juliet, she was always in the kitchen, her bedroom, or her attic office. But since Dad . . . well, she could be really quiet sometimes.

And sometimes she didn't seem to hear me. Sometimes I felt like I was the mom. Sometimes I reminded her to eat dinner and to go to bed, and sometimes I even curled next to her in bed so that I could pull up the covers over us both. It didn't happen as much now, though. Every day, she acted more *Mom* Mom.

I rolled the bike down the porch and strapped on my helmet.

"Where are you going?" Min popped out from behind the bushes that separated our houses.

I yelped and dropped my bike onto my foot. "What are you doing scaring a person like that?"

Min crossed her arms. Though it was barely eight in the morning, she was completely put together in orange capri pants with a white shirt that had bows on the sleeves. She wore an orange ruffled headband and orange shoestrings in her white sneakers. "I'm waiting for you to come outside," she said. "You're my very best friend in the world, and I haven't seen you in days."

"Oh, that's really nice—"

"And I need to tell you that you're being mean to Gordon. It's not his fault that he was there at the perfect time, but it *was* super smart of him to start taking pictures instead of screaming or running away. And that's why Ellen thinks he's cool and why CNN wants to profile his superior journalism. But you? *You're* deciding to be a real jerk about it."

"I am *not* being a jerk!" I bent to retrieve my bike. "I simply think we need to move forward."

"No, you're being *jealous*." Min put her hands on the handlebars of the bike, locking me in place.

"I am not jealous." I laughed.

"Then why are you laughing like that?"

"Like what? This is my natural laugh." I did it again. "Ha! Hahaha! Ha!"

Min crossed her arms and sighed. "That is not how you laugh. You laugh out of your nose like a cat with allergies."

"That is *not* true. Now you're being the jerk!" I pushed the bike toward her, and she shoved it back.

A satisfied smile spread across Min's face. "So, you admit that you were being a jerk. Good."

"No! I—" Too angry to continue, I adjusted my helmet. "Okay, fine. I could've handled that whole Gordon thing better."

Min's bottom lip puckered out, and she nodded. "Good job."

"At what?"

"Admitting you were wrong. Now you need to apologize to Gordon." She patted my helmeted head. "I'll go with you now. Maybe Ellen's there." She smoothed her hair.

"I have to go cover another story. Like it or not, this isn't the only news in town."

"Well, it's the main story in the *Burlington Meadows Journal*'s editorial." Min smirked when I gasped; she loved knowing things I didn't.

"What editorial?"

"The one that reporter guy wrote. Randolph Yellow. He says . . ." Min stiffened and made her voice deep: "*The death of small-town newspapers is leading to reputable news sources being passed over in favor of juvenile attempts. Kids, who should be spending their summers building forts and selling lemonade, are instead masquerading as the press. The results could be disastrous.*"

"Is that paraphrasing or did you memorize it?"

"You're not the only one with a photographic memory. It only took sixteen readings to remember it."

"That's not photographic."

Min shrugged. "Still counts."

"No, it doesn't. It literally does not count."

"Don't be so literal."

I pushed past her. I'd deal with the editorial later. For now, I had a story to pursue.

"Where are you going? Maybe I'll come along," Min said as though I had invited her.

"I'm going to go up to the edge of town and talk to a lonely old woman about her pen."

"Actually, I'm busy," Min said and skipped back to her house.

———————————————

This time, the trip to Ms. Wilkonson's didn't seem nearly as long, probably since I knew where I was going. Maybe also because I spent the whole time thinking about what I would say to Gordon when I saw him next. I had a speech ready. *Gordon, I'm sorry for my reaction. I'm really glad you were where I had assigned you to be when the news broke about the burglar, and I'm really happy that you learned about being a journalist from me so quickly and were able to capture those images. I'm also really glad that you're getting the attention we deserve for that hard work.*

It might need tweaking.

Ms. Wilkonson was expecting me. I spotted her rocking in a chair on the front porch. When I pedaled down the driveway, she stood and watched me.

"I knew you'd be back," she said.

"Well, I told you I'd be here. My mom called you. And you left me all of those messages. . . ."

"I just have to know: Who told you about the pen?" Ms. Wilkonson bopped on the balls of her feet, reminding me of Min, who also tended to do things like that. I hoped she also didn't dot her i's with hearts the way Min did.

"Um . . . you did." I got off the bike and laid it on the grass.

Two red circles bloomed on Ms. Wilkonson's cheeks. She was tall and thin, and her skin was as pale as Charlotte's. I wondered if her hair had also once been red before it had turned white.

"Right, but you showed up here. It was because of the pen, right?"

I turned to the side as I took off my helmet. I didn't want to admit that the rest of the news staff had dared me to find a story at a random spot on the Bear Creek map and that's how I ended up at her door. Somehow, I doubted that would lead to Ms. Wilkonson sharing a whole lot with me. But on the other hand, journalistic ethics demanded honesty. "Well, our newspaper is young—"

Ms. Wilkonson snorted, which was unnecessary. "Yes, I read in the *Journal* this morning about how young your paper is."

"So," I continued, trying to ignore how it sounded as if she had put quote marks around the word *paper*, "we're reaching throughout the community for people's stories."

Ms. Wilkonson's eyes narrowed. "You just rode all the way up Morgan Road on your bike on the chance that you could find a story?"

I pulled out my pen and notebook from my back pocket.

"You're an odd child."

"My dad says I'm highly intelligent and socially awkward."

"As am I," she said.

"That explains a lot." We both nodded.

Ms. Wilkonson stood and held open the screen door. "Come on in, then."

———————————

About an hour later, I checked my notes. "Okay, so the governor signed this bill and gave you the pen?"

"Right," Ms. Wilkonson said. We were sitting at her kitchen table. She had pushed a bunch of papers and books to the side and poured each of us a glass of lemonade. She nudged a little plate full of cookies in my direction.

Dad once had to have a stern conversation with a reporter who had been gifted with a painting by an artist he had profiled. The journalist was angry that Dad asked him to pay the artist if he intended to keep the piece or to donate it to a charity. *A hallmark of ethical journalism is that our coverage is independent of influence,* Dad told me.

I eyed the cookies. I was pretty sure they weren't a gift meant to influence my coverage of the story. If so, they'd probably at least have chocolate chips, not raisins. I took one from the plate and nibbled as I reviewed my notes.

"And the bill declared that people who donated their land to a trust that promised not to cut down the trees wouldn't have to pay taxes on the land?"

"Right." Ms. Wilkonson sat back in her seat and smiled.

I blinked at her. "Okay. But why?"

"Well, taxes are quite expensive, Nellie." Ms. Wilkonson took a bite of a cookie, made a face, and put it back on her plate. "Should've used chocolate chips. I'm not sure how old these raisins are."

"Why was that important to you?"

"Well, it shouldn't be, I suppose. Raisins are dried up grapes, so I guess old raisins are just extra dried."

"No," I said, "I mean, the land trust thing. Why was it important to you that it be easier to donate to trusts?"

Ms. Wilkonson stared at her plate for a long moment. "Follow me."

CHAPTER SEVEN

I GASPED WHEN MS. Wilkonson opened the back door. While the inside of her house was cluttered with piles of papers, books, and junk that she didn't seem to know what to do with, the backyard was a paradise. A stone patio spread out from the sliding back door into a large oval. Surrounding it were layers of flowering plants—lilies, hydrangeas, roses, daisies, and more that I couldn't name. They weren't like the flower gardens in Mrs. Kim-Franklin's pristine yard, where each plant was perfectly round with three inches of mulch boundary between it and the next one. These gardens seemed to spill right out from the surrounding forest, growing as easily into and over each other as if one day it had rained seeds.

"Wow," I whispered.

Ms. Wilkonson, who had been stiff and almost impossible to get a story out of inside her cluttered, cramped kitchen, let out a long exhale. She winked and pointed to a tall plant with a spiky hot pink ball growing at the top. A shimmery hummingbird dipped in and out of the plant. "Bee balm," she said softly. "The hummingbird is there every morning. Sometimes it gets mixed up and comes when another hummingbird visits. Then they fight, which is a terrifying, beautiful sight, those long sword-like beaks dipping and pecking."

It was hard for me to imagine the busy, beautiful bird being angry about sharing.

"You know how it is," Ms. Wilkonson shrugged, "when people get it into their heads about how things should be."

"Is this what you wanted to show me?" I asked. A trio of chipmunks raced across the patio, nearly over my feet. I was a city girl, but I could've spent all day standing on that patio, listening to the birds and gazing at the flowers.

"Not exactly." Ms. Wilkonson strode across the stones to a narrow path that led into the woods. Along the way, she stopped and plucked a few wild raspberries from a bush. "Be careful of the thorns."

I nabbed one, giving the briars a lot of extra space. The berry was so sweet and fresh—almost as good as Miss Juliet's ice cream—that I pulled another and another. When I looked up, Ms. Wilkonson was disappearing into the trees. I trotted toward her. The dense foliage dimmed the sunlight, and the trees' canopy made the air cool enough that my T-shirt loosened from where it had been sticking to my back. The spots on my neck that no longer had hair plastered to them tickled with the breeze. Under our feet was a carpet of fallen needles and browning leaves. The trees, a mixture of towering pines and widespread maples and oaks, swayed as we walked. A large bird, probably a hawk, swooped overhead. I stepped closer to Ms. Wilkonson when I heard a rustling on the ground to my left.

"Don't worry," she said with a laugh. "It's just a squirrel."

Suddenly, the woods opened up and there lay nothing but wide, frothy ferns and a few tiny saplings. The air dampened and warmed. While steps earlier the sky had been filled with the chittering of squirrels and rustles from critters running through the woods, now the only birdsong came from the periphery of the clearing.

Ms. Wilkonson took a deep breath. "My husband cleared this plot more than twenty years ago. He wanted to parcel up our land—we had two hundred acres—into housing developments. Was going to fit in fifty houses by the time he was done. Maybe more. This was going to be the spot for the first house. A road would've gone through our front yard to the house back here, straight through the garden. He said it would make us richer than we could imagine."

She ran her hands over the tops of the ferns, which reached just above her knees. "Our daughter was about to go to college. We didn't think we had enough money to pay the tuition, not with how much we spent on taxes every year for the land. Divvying up the plot into homes was going to pay for it. He had it all worked out."

I looked around at the bare patch in the forest and gulped down the image of Ms. Wilkonson's garden being run through by an asphalt road.

"What happened?" I hadn't even realized my notebook was open and in my hand until I started writing notes.

Ms. Wilkonson stood, her back still toward me. "I said no, didn't I?" She looked up at the sky and I realized how warm it was in the barren area. "This land had been my papa's. He left it to me to do with what I wanted. I played here as a child. Once, when I was about your age, it stormed suddenly, and I ran through the woods. Royally lost for a day and a half. I followed deer trails home, straight to the hostas my mama had planted in the side yard. She never complained about the deer gnawing them to stalks again."

She turned back toward me. "As my husband platted houses on this land, working with contractors to figure out cheap supplies and architects who promised quick builds, I contacted land trusts. I worked with them to make it possible for me to give them the land. To keep it like it is now, wild and free.

"I had dreams that one day my daughter would have her own children, and they'd play here, too, turning fallen trees into playgrounds. Climbing pines 'til they rocked back and forth the way she had. Sleeping on that patio on hot summer nights, watching the moonlit bats catch mosquitos in the sky."

"Did he know you were doing that?" I asked. "Going to the land trust while he talked to contractors?"

Her shoulders peaked and fell. "No. Outside of the house, I was brave. I campaigned so hard. I joined the land trusts. Going out in public . . ." She shuddered. "It's not exactly easy for me. Talking in public—it's not something that I want. I'd rather be here, in this house." She laughed. "I mean, these woods. The house, not so much. But I wasn't brave enough to tell him."

I sat down on a stump, my hand scrawling across the pages, capturing her exact quotes. "How did he find out?"

"The same day I saw the trucks going across the yard and the trees being felled in this patch. Up until then, everything was just talk, you know. We'd sit on that porch, waiting for our daughter to get home from a date or from working at the ice cream shop, and he'd talk about turning the forest into a neighborhood. I'd talk about our grandchildren playing in the woods." She took a deep breath. "He'd tell me about who he talked to that day, contractors and whatnot, and I'd talk about the land trusts working to preserve Bear Creek."

"You argued about it?"

"No." She shook her head. "We never fought. Just talked. Side by side, but totally different conversations. Not hearing what the other person was saying." For some reason, that made me think of Dad. The discussions we used to have on the swings, when I'd talk and talk and talk, and he'd just listen. Had he been sharing, too? Had I just not been listening?

The trunks of the trees in the surrounding woods felt like they were a silent audience as Ms. Wilkonson stood in the middle of a rustling green stage of ferns. For just a second, and maybe it was because of the sunlight shimmering over her, I pictured what she had looked like as a girl.

"I felt so useful, you know? I had gone to college, but never went to law school as I had intended. I had missed my corner of Bear Creek too much. How relieved I was that my husband was willing to move here, commuting every day to Burlington Meadows. He'd lament that Susie, our girl, had to go so far to play with friends, but I knew the woods would be there for her. What kind of childhood would it be without trees?"

I bit my lip to keep from talking about the city, how *that* had been a wonderful place to grow up. I had learned so much about people and independence thanks to my parents raising me with a subway pass and an endless stream of parks and concerts, restaurants and museums. But this was an interview, not a conversation.

"He seemed surprised when I told him I was going all the way to Augusta with the land trust for the day. But he didn't talk me out of it. He said he was making progress with the land development idea, and I didn't think to ask what that meant. Everything was still so theoretical. Once it was signed, once the governor made it official that any donated land could be tax exempt, I was going to tell him about the money we'd save by donating our land—a donation that would make it easier for Susie to get student loans. Between those loans and our nest egg, she'd be secure. I had no idea that the same day, he'd invest our savings into creating the first model home."

Ms. Wilkonson took a deep breath, then told me about the grandeur of the governor's office. She said her husband would've loved it, all of the press and attention. How she, for the first time ever, felt part of a group. How she enjoyed the laughter and cheers as the governor handed her the pen that changed everything—that made everything go from a concept to a reality. How she was so moved by the moment that she went straight to the trust and used the same pen to sign over all but ten of those acres to the trust.

How she was still working out how exactly she'd tell her husband she had made her plans a reality and that his would have to shift. How she had come home to find tracks through her yard that had destroyed her mother's lilies.

———————

"But how could you have signed over the land without your husband's signature too? Wasn't half the land his?" I asked.

Ms. Wilkonson bowed her head for a second. "It was my family's land. I had control of it. Or at least I thought I did.

We had a difficult conversation when I got back. I ordered the trucks off the property. This plot was all that they had managed to clear. Jerry and I talked the night through. Maybe for the first time, we actually heard each other."

She sat on the stump next to me. "He left the next night. Susie went with him. I tried again and again to tell them that I did this for us, that the land would be ours. It'd be here forever, for generations. But all Jerry heard was that I had gone behind his back. And all Susie heard was that I had squandered her inheritance. All my words felt sticky as sap."

Ms. Wilkonson pressed her hand to her cheek. "But it's still here. It's still right here." She stood and put her hands on her hips. "Someday the forest will patch this bare spot."

I sat on a stump, writing notes and wondering what to ask next.

Ms. Wilkonson turned in a small circle. "One day, just a couple hours really, and everything changed. Everything I thought I knew was gone. Everything I thought I had, fell with the trees in this clearing. Did you know things could change that quickly?"

I stood, again biting down my own stories. I stifled my own memories. *Dad leaving that morning. "See you later,*

Cub!" The knock at the door that afternoon. The police officer asking to talk with Mom. There's been an accident. The sound she made.

"Yes. I know," was all I said.

Ms. Wilkonson stared at the ferns. "The trust members, they stayed with me through everything. You wouldn't believe all that they've accomplished, all they've managed to do because of that legislation."

In my notebook, I wrote *Talk to the Trust!* in red ink so I'd remember to follow up with members about the significance of Ms. Wilkonson's efforts. The letters blurred as I swiped at my eyes. *C'mon, Nellie,* I told myself. I had to focus on Ms. Wilkonson's story, not the ones her questions triggered in me.

Ms. Wilkonson clasped her hands together in front of her. "What you asked earlier, about whether the land was mine to give away? We hashed that out. Eventually, Jerry was given half the land. He took the part closest to town. There's a posh neighborhood there now, from what I hear."

I closed my eyes, picturing the map of Bear Creek. I knew the area she meant, the fancier part of town. The houses there were all two stories tall and brick, with careful patches of square plots. It looked like a different planet than the aging farmhouses in the rest of Bear Creek. "Foxcroft Estates, right? My friend Gordon lives there. I think Charlotte might, too."

Ms. Wilkonson's nose wrinkled. "Did you say Charlotte?"

I nodded. "Yeah, she's part of the Newspaper Club."

"I think it's time you went home."

"But—"

"I think you have everything you need to know."

"Is this about Charlotte?"

"That's quite enough." She crossed her arms. "I'm tired. It's time for you to leave."

With that she strode back down the path. In the distance, I heard the slam of her back door.

I walked around front to my bicycle, thinking about Ms. Wilkonson's story and trying to figure out how I'd write it and what had gone wrong at the end. Why I had ever thought of this as a story about a silly pen when the fact was everything about it was so jumbled and complicated?

But Ms. Wilkonson's story? That wasn't the only complicated story I'd face that day. Instead, I'd find one mess after another on the way home.

CHAPTER EIGHT

I CHECKED MY PHONE before I left Ms. Wilkonson's house. No missed calls or texts from Mom or the Cubs. I checked my email, too, just to make sure *Ellen* hadn't messaged me. Nothing, except for a couple messages from people in town. I quickly read them, hoping for a story lead. Instead, one pointed out that kids should be playing baseball in the summer, not going to crime scenes. Another asked if *The Cub Report* covered playtimes at the park. They clearly didn't get it.

I tightened my helmet, hopped on my bike, and headed down Ms. Wilkonson's driveway. "Bye!" I called out as

I passed the screen door. "I'll let you know if I have any follow-up questions!"

She didn't reply. I shrugged, trying to puzzle out why she had suddenly stopped sharing her story. As I headed down the hill toward Bear Creek, I thought about the holes I'd need to fill in the story. I'd need to contact the land trust to find out more about the bill Ms. Wilkonson campaigned so hard to get passed. I'd need to learn more about how it had affected Bear Creek and ripped her family apart.

And suddenly I felt angry. Ms. Wilkonson had stood in that bare patch in the forest talking about how things had changed so quickly, how her daughter no longer spoke with her, how her husband had left. But they were still *here*. Her daughter was somewhere she could reach. Ms. Wilkonson could go to her, see her. She could talk to her and have her talk back. She could touch her. She could hug her again. She could tell her she loved her and hear her say it back, right out loud.

But instead, she stood in the middle of those ferns, grew those spilled-over lilies, or rocked alone on that porch meant for a whole family. She just was waiting for someone to stop by so she could justify boxing up that silly pen instead of making up with her family.

I turned around and before I knew it, I was back on Ms. Wilkonson's porch. *This is just a question for the article,* I told myself. *This is being a good reporter, asking the tough questions.* Dad's face flashed in front of me, and my stomach squished and boiled. I knocked on the screen door, but Ms. Wilkonson didn't come to answer. I knew she was in there; I could hear a creaking step from the kitchen. "Why don't you tell her?" I shouted into the cluttered house. "Why don't you go to Susie and tell her why you did what you did? Why don't you *fix* it?"

Ms. Wilkonson didn't reply. She didn't move. Maybe I was wrong, maybe she wasn't in there.

I turned to go down the porch steps but then heard her approaching. She stood just inside the screen door. "What if I can't explain it right so they'd understand?"

"They don't understand now," I said. "But they'd have a better shot at it if you told them. Right now, I bet they think you love that silly pen more than you love them." I took a deep breath. That hadn't been neutral or being a good journalist. "Not that your pen is silly. Your pen is . . . cool. I guess."

Ms. Wilkonson grimaced. Then she said, "I need to think about it."

"Twenty years isn't enough time to think?" I clenched my teeth together to keep from saying any more.

"This was a mistake," Ms. Wilkonson said. "I'm not sure I want an article anymore."

———————————————————

I pedaled carefully down the hill, using the handbrakes frequently. I felt like Ms. Wilkonson's story and how much I missed Dad had been rolled up into one big cotton ball, and here I was trying to pull the wispy threads apart into two separate piles.

If Ms. Wilkonson refused future interviews, I might not be able to write the article. She knew I was a reporter and hadn't said the interview was off the record (something I could not use in an article), so I *could* still use all of my notes. Her saying she didn't want an article to be written couldn't stop me from using what she had already shared. But the information I had wasn't a complete picture. And it wasn't like it was breaking news; if she didn't want an article, there wasn't a compelling reason to push for it.

Except, of course, for the fact that we didn't have any other stories for the next *Cub Report*. And the fact that Charlotte, Gloria, and Min had dared me to prove that everybody has a story.

"So, what do you think, Dad?" I asked out loud. It was getting harder to hear him. *Follow the story.* I don't know if it was in Dad's voice or mine, but it seemed like good advice. "Okay." I exhaled. "I'll follow the story. Anything else?"

"Yow."

That definitely wasn't Dad's voice.

I stopped the bike, planting my feet on either side. "Yow!" I heard again, coming not from my mind but from a briar bush. I bent and peered under the tangle of thorns and branches.

"Oh, I know what that's like," I said to the two tiny green eyes blinking back at me. "Do you need help?" I asked the kitten.

"Yow." That sounded a whole lot like a yes.

———

At the bottom of the hill, I felt my phone vibrate with messages. But I was too busy cradling a squirming kitten inside my helmet with one hand and directing my bicycle with the other.

The kitten was only slightly bigger than my hand, all gray and black with green eyes. She rubbed her face into my knuckles as I held the helmet, but she dug her razor-sharp claws in my skin if I tried to carry her. While none of the briars stuck to her fur, I did have a few more in my hair. Mom probably wasn't going to be happy about that.

I knew I should visit the land trust offices, but I had to get Woodward home and settled. That's was the kitten's name. If she lived with journalists, she had to have a strong journalist's name, and Bob Woodward was one of the best.

Dad had told me bedtime stories about Bob Woodward and Carl Bernstein, the *Washington Post* reporters whose diligence in reporting a burglary attempt of the Democratic National Committee headquarters at a hotel called the Watergate led to investigations that revealed President Richard Nixon's involvement. The president resigned and Woodward and Bernstein were lauded as among the best journalists in the world, right up there with Nellie Bly.

Maybe some people would think Woodward wasn't a good name for a kitten, but they were wrong. Fact: Woodward wasn't afraid to work hard. That was important because Woodward and I had to convince Mom she belonged with us. Besides, what did cats care about things like names?

This made me wonder what *did* concern cats. I wasn't exactly an animal person. Alejandro—who once told me I didn't know how to have fun—spent a lot of time taking his dog for walks and then coming home carrying little bags filled with poop. Once his snake slithered out of its tank and was finally found a few days later in an apartment across the hall, trapped inside a hamster cage, too swollen from swallowing Pigsy the hamster to get back out. Both of those situations seemed decidedly not-fun to me.

I stared at Woodward. She yowed back at me. When Mom was a girl, she had had a cat. Its name was Peanut Butter and she slept on Mom's bed. Having a cat curled up in the groove between my shoulder and my ear sounded pretty nice. I bet it would make falling asleep a lot easier than staring up at the blobby, fading glow-in-the-dark stars whoever had last used my bedroom had stuck on the ceiling.

But maybe Woodward belonged to someone else. Maybe they were looking for her right now. Woodward twisted her head so my knuckle rubbed the velvety spot just behind her ear. She was so soft. Soon her little eyes closed and a quiet rumble echoed through her body. I'd put some posters up at the diner and the park just in case someone was looking for her. But I really hoped she could be mine. Her small paws opened and closed as she snoozed. Something squishy fluttered in my heart.

"Listen, Woodward," I said as I walked the bike down the street toward my house. She opened one eye. "You're going to need to be quiet now and extra, extra cute later when I reveal you to Mom." There was a car in the driveway, so with any luck Mom would be distracted by a guest and I could sneak Woodward up to my room where she would silently hide as I prepared a PowerPoint presentation on the benefits of childhood pets.

Once I was at the edge of my yard, I recognized the car; it was Dr. Burke's. I squelched the uncomfortable flash of jealousy that burned in my chest at thinking of Gordon. That quickly warped into a new feeling—excitement. Because maybe, just maybe, Dr. Burke was here with Gordon to hash out plans with Mom for our upcoming appearance on *Ellen*. Maybe they were in there, right now, sitting around the kitchen table celebrating the First Amendment and the girl (*me!*) who inspired Gordon to be so successful.

I tucked my T-shirt into my shorts and then dropped Woodward inside the shirt. With any luck, I could sneak past Mom and Dr. Burke, untuck my shirt, drop Woodward onto my bed, dart back down the stairs, and await the glorious news that I would soon be on *Ellen*.

CHAPTER NINE

I DANCED A LITTLE as I skipped up to the back door, practicing how I would make my entrance on the show. A little shuffle, shuffle, wiggle, wiggle. The audience would love that.

Woodward, stashed inside my T-shirt, did not. She yowed again and I felt either tiny teeth or tiny claws swipe at my belly. I cradled the little kitten lump with my hand and refocused. *Get upstairs, hide Woodward, back to Mom.*

Mom and Dr. Burke were talking in the living room, which was convenient because it gave me ample time to sneak up the stairs but also strange because Mom never sat in the living room. We spent almost all our time in the kitchen. Every time anyone had come over (which was usually just Mrs. Kim-Franklin, since she and Mom were best friends since college), Mom served mugs of tea in the kitchen. Except now, the teapot was on the kitchen table and they were in the living room.

Dr. Burke and Mom were talking in the super-polite way two adults who don't know each other well talk. "I'm confident all of your concerns are unfounded," Mom said. *Huh.* I guessed maybe Dr. Burke had some reservations about *Ellen.*

Next to the teapot was a copy of the *Journal.* It was folded back to show the editorial Min had partially memorized. I paused to scan before sneaking over to the stairway.

The editorial, or opinion piece, was titled, *Leave the reporting to the pros.* I rolled my eyes. I had *tried* to give the Bear Creek stories to the professionals; the local newspaper had shuttered. Under the editorial was a column, an opinion piece written by a newspaper staff member. I recognized the mugshot as Randolph Yellow, the snotty reporter who had acted like we weren't real reporters the day Gordon busted the criminal. The headline read: *Children should be playing, not reporting.* The paragraph Min had recited from memory was pulled out and in large italics. Swallowing down another growl, I shoved the paper under my T-shirt next to Woodward.

I tiptoed through the kitchen toward the staircase with one hand cradling Woodward through my T-shirt.

"I will do what I have to do to keep my son safe," Dr. Burke said. "Our parenting styles are clearly not in sync."

I paused, a foot on the bottom stair. Part of me screamed to stick to the plan. Most of me was glued in place, pondering what Dr. Burke was saying.

Mom cleared her throat. *Uh-oh.* She only made that noise when she was about to launch into a what-were-you-thinking conversation. "Our styles might differ—I, for example, respect my child's autonomy and independence, whereas you appear to be more interested in controlling your son's behavior—but I promise you, the Newspaper Club is a safe pastime."

"Safe?" Dr. Burke said, her voice still polite. She laughed once. "How long did you study journalism?"

"I studied for four years at Penn State and interned for a year after that."

"Yet you think a bunch of ten- to twelve-year-olds can take on the same work? You read that article—children should be spending their summer playing, not trying to steal the jobs of professionals."

"It wasn't an article; it was a *column*," Mom corrected. "Simply an opinion piece. And what Nellie and the rest of the

Cubs are doing is solid work, regardless of their age. They most certainly didn't *steal* a single person's job; the town's newspaper folded because too few of us journalists have the support of the community. What they're doing is commendable and will make them literate in what constitutes quality media and productive members of our society."

"But where does it put them in the meantime?" I heard a shuffle, probably Dr. Burke shifting in her seat. "Have you figured out where Nellie is yet?"

Oh, no!

"I'm well aware that Nellie is working on a story and will be home, safe and sound, at any moment," Mom snapped.

"But she hasn't responded to your texts?" Dr. Burke asked.

As if on cue, my phone buzzed again in my pocket. Because one leg was up on the stairs and the other on the kitchen floor, the phone slipped out of my pocket. I saw the phone drop as if in slow motion to the wooden step and land on its side with a clatter. I lunged to grab it. That sound or maybe the squishing startled Woodward, who gave the biggest *YOW!* I'd ever heard and tried to claw her way through my shirt. I screamed, sounding a whole lot like Woodward, as her nails slashed up my chest. I fell backward down the step onto my bottom with a thump.

Mom and Dr. Burke both gasped and soon there they were in front of me. Sitting at the bottom of the stairs like that, I had a great view of not only both adults but of the big mirror hanging over the couch.

I was sprawled out on the floor, hair once again filled with briars, the top of my head covered by a kitten with fur raised and tail whipping.

"Hi, Mom," I managed. "I'm home."

"*Nellie Marguerite Murrow,*" Mom hissed. Dr. Burke crossed her arms and raised an eyebrow. "Your hair! What am I going to do with you? And is that a *cat*? Have you stolen *another* cat?"

"First of all, I did not *steal* Fluff. Next, can we ignore Woodward for a second? I was going to prepare a PowerPoint presentation before introducing her." The kitten hopped from my head and curled onto my lap, her head on my knee. "Can we keep her?" I squeaked.

"Nellie," Mom sighed my name. "You know your dad is allergic—" She stopped what she was going to say and covered her mouth with her hands.

Dad's allergic to cats. That's why we never had one, even with Mom's stories about Peanut Butter. How could I have forgotten? That's how he had discovered Fluff—because he couldn't stop sneezing when he passed my bedroom. For some silly reason, the idea that we *could* have a cat now because we didn't have him made me feel . . . I don't know how it made me feel. But it did make tears bloom in my eyes.

Dr. Burke's hands dropped to her sides. "Let's get that hair taken care of, Nellie." She reached down for my hand and helped me stand. Then she wrapped an arm around my shoulder. Her voice was gentle as she said, "Why don't you have a seat in the kitchen, and I'll see what I can do?"

Woodward meowed and Dr. Burke smiled at her. She had a smile just like Gordon's. "Let's get this little one some milk while we're at it." As we passed Mom, still frozen with her hands covering her mouth, Dr. Burke reached out with her other hand and squeezed Mom's shoulder.

———

About a half hour later, Woodward was napping peacefully on the floor after lapping up a shallow bowl of milk. Dr. Burke told me what I'd need to get to keep Woodward safe—a collar, a litter box, and some kitten chow from the pet shop downtown. She also gave me the name of a veterinarian. All the while, her fingers gently pulled the briars from my hair. It wasn't as bad this time. We only had to use the scissors twice. Both of those were for chunks of hair in the front of my head, though, so combined with the missing pieces in the back, I needed to invest in hats.

By the time Dr. Burke pulled the last briar out of my hair, Mom was sitting next to us at the table, occasionally bending down to rub Woodward behind the ears.

Dr. Burke smoothed my hair and turned toward Mom. "Listen, I know you both have been through a lot. I will be there for you in any way I can. I truly mean that. But Gordon can no longer be part of *The Cub Report*."

"But—" I started.

She silenced me with an upturned eyebrow. "I do not support organizations for children without adult guidance." She sat across from Mom and folded her hands on the tabletop. "School begins next week. Let's discuss creating a school-sponsored newspaper club."

"No!" I gasped, startling Woodward, who yawned and trotted over to me. I scooped her up to my lap. "A newspaper's independence is key to its success."

"Lots of school newspapers are very successful." Dr. Burke took a deep breath. "And they wouldn't require a young boy to track a desperate escaped convict." She peered straight into my eyes. "My son is getting a whole lot of praise for a photograph he never should've been in a position to take. Have you thought about what would've happened if that man had a weapon? Or even if he didn't, what if he *had* made it out of that window?" She leaned forward. "Have you considered the flip side to all of this attention Gordon is getting?"

"What do you mean?" asked Mom, her face pale.

"That convicted felon is also getting a lot of attention. A lot of *negative* attention. I bet he's pretty rankled at a certain twelve-year-old boy right now. And he escaped prison once. What if he does it again? What if he's still angry after his time is served? What might he be plotting while Gordon's phone pings with offers to go on talk shows and as his photo is turned into memes online?"

I lowered my head, thinking hard. I hadn't considered any of those concerns. I had only been thinking about the newspaper. I had only been thinking about myself.

"This is what's keeping me up at night lately," Dr. Burke said. "That and Gordon's nightmares, but I doubt he's shared any of those with you, either."

"I didn't know . . ."

She took another deep breath. "Gordon is no longer allowed to be part of *The Cub Report*, not that he asked for permission initially. Furthermore, I don't think *any* of you should be doing this. It's far too dangerous."

———————————

After Dr. Burke left, Mom and I sat at the table in silence. Mom suddenly propped up her head on her hands. "I need to tell you I'm sorry."

"What?" I sat back in my chair. Of all the things I thought she'd say to me after I had been caught sneaking up the stairs, covered in briars and holding a cat, this was not on the list.

"Since your dad died, I haven't been present. It's like I'm moving through this cloud, just waiting for it to lift so I can see things crisply." She shook her head, as if batting the cloud side to side. Her hair was beginning to slip from the topknot. She sat back and fidgeted with a corner of her T-shirt. It was a Pink Floyd one that had belonged to Dad. Mom used to wear tailored button-down shirts and slacks. I pressed my lips together, not wanting to hear what she was saying but also needing to hear it. "That hasn't been fair to you."

"Mom, I—"

She held up her hand to quiet me. "I'm doing the best I can. I can tell you that, and I know you know it. But it doesn't change the fact that I am still your mother, and as your mom, I should be more on top of where you are and what you're doing."

"Please don't make me download that creepy app that Min has on her phone. The one where you can see a satellite image of me at all times."

Mom laughed. "I'm just saying that I should be aware. I knew you were covering a story today, but I didn't know the first time you rode your bike out there, and that's not safe." She sat back in her seat. "If *The Cub Report* is going to continue, we need to hash out some ground rules."

"If?" I repeated.

"We," she said, "also need to discuss this cat."

"Woodward," I mumbled, as I lifted the fur ball from my lap to face her. Mom's mouth twitched when I said her name.

"Let's get Woodward checked out by the vet." She rubbed the kitten between the ears. Maybe that acknowledgment that keeping her was a possibility should've filled me with joy, but I was too snared by that *if*. If The Cub Report *is going to continue*. Was it falling apart? Was it really too dangerous for kids, even smart, experienced ones, to report the news?

The editorial from the *Burlington Meadows Journal* lay on the table in front of me.

As Mom dialed the veterinarian on her phone, I called the phone number on the editorial page of the *Journal*. "Hello, this is Nellie Murrow. I'd like to report a correction. Randolph Yellow's column regarding *The Cub Report* says that the newspaper is run by, quote, 'a bunch of twelve-year-olds.' I'm eleven. Our graphic designer is ten."

After being assured the newspaper would run a correction in the next issue, I typed a text out to the staff: *Emergency meeting at the newsroom.*

CHAPTER TEN

WOODWARD AND I WERE the first in the newsroom, except for Stuff. The goat sniffed a little at Woodward, and then they both lay down in the hay. After a few moments, Thom's back door opened and closed. Another sound carried over the music his moms play all of the time; it sounded a lot like Woodward, but she was still snuggled against the goat.

I was about to ask Thom about it when someone else arrived—Gordon.

"Hey!" I rushed over to him. "Your mom said—"

"I know what my mom said." Gordon dropped his skateboard. "She's been saying it nonstop to me ever since our special edition. But I'm here."

"Gordon, I'm sorry," I said. "I was a jerk and I was . . ." Some words feel stickier than bubble gum. "I was jealous, I guess. Getting that picture was awesome journalism and you deserve all the praise for it."

I gave him a hug, then jumped backward because I am not the type to give hugs, especially to cute boys. "Look," I said to avoid talking about the hug. I pointed to Woodward. "We have a new staff member."

Woodward was curled on Gordon's shoulder when Gloria and Charlotte arrived. Gloria was in her diner shirt. "I only have a minute and then I've got to get back to work. I've been gone too much for this newspaper stuff. Dad's been interviewing waitresses."

"Isn't that a good thing?" Charlotte asked. "Doesn't that mean you'll be able to work fewer hours?"

Gloria shook her head, making the beads in her hair click. "Maybe if we could afford another employee, her benefits and all of that. We can't." Her chin lifted. "I can manage more than he thinks I can. I just have to prove that to Dad." Gloria dropped her arms and made a face. "Besides, I don't like her. Dad sure seems to, though."

"Oh," Charlotte said.

I moved closer to Charlotte. "Hey," I whispered to her, "after the meeting, we should talk. Ms. Wilkonson acted really odd when I mentioned you."

Now Charlotte's face turned flame red. "Why would you mention me?" She shoved her book into her bag and shouldered it. "I have to go, too."

"Wait!" I called out. "Hold on!"

Min stomped into the barn, practically knocking into Charlotte. Min's face was streaked with tears. "Mom says I have to quit."

"What?" I yelped. "What do you mean?"

"First that *kids should be playing, not reporting* article—"

"*Column*," Gloria, Gordon, and Thom all corrected at once, making my heart swell despite the panic at losing our graphic designer.

Min waved her hands. "Whatever. Then Dr. Burke talked with her about how dangerous it is for us to be journalists— that it's one of the most dangerous professions in the United States. I told her, 'I don't go out there covering stories, coming back covered in briars, and sneaking into the house holding a cat; I design the stories inside our house or at the barn next door. But she wouldn't listen to me."

"Min, were you spying on me again?" I patted down what remained of my hair.

Min continued as if I hadn't spoken. "And then Mom told me that she read our email—do any of the rest of you check it?—and there was a message from the Associated Press, and they want to do a profile of us."

I gasped and Gordon pumped the air. "That's awesome!" Gloria said. I looked around for Charlotte, forgetting she left just before Min's announcement.

"Yeah, I thought it was awesome, too, but it's not. The reporter says she wants to write about us following convicts around and, from the last issue, saving old ladies. And that's why I have to quit!" Min's hands curled into fists as she continued. "Mom said, 'I don't think it's appropriate for little girls' habits to be profiled in newspapers.'" Min's voice turned high-pitched as she imitated Mrs. Kim-Franklin's tone. "But then Dad said"—and here Min's voice turned deep—"'Oh, what's the harm? They're just doing a little Bear Creek paper.' And I told him, 'Journalism is *my life*! It's important!' Mom said, 'No! *Safety* is important.' She says Dr. Burke told her that at next week's school board meeting, she's going to propose a supervised school paper so that we aren't necessary anymore. I ran across the street to be here because we *should* be in the Associated Press. And my picture should, too, right in the middle. I might not be hanging out with pigs or covered in briars and holding diseased-looking cats, but what I do is still journalism. No one would even read the paper if it weren't for my designs! I'll wear my dress with pink—"

"Ruffles," I finished for her. "Yeah, we know. But we need to talk about this. We need to talk about all of this." I took a deep breath. "Being in the AP would be great, but it's also a distraction. All of this attention we're getting for one lucky photograph is compromising our credibility. I don't know if that silly photo is worth—"

"Silly? Lucky?" Gordon snapped. "What?"

"I didn't mean—"

"Do you have any idea how hard it's been on me since that *silly* photo was printed? How *unlucky* it's been?"

Without meaning to, I snorted. Everyone looked at me, so I shrugged. "It's just it hasn't exactly been *hard*, has it? All of that attention? *Ellen* calling you?"

Gordon stood and put Woodward on the hay bale in front of him. Woodward pawed at the air between them as if offended by the change in circumstance. "That's what this is about? You're jealous?" Gordon shook his head. "You *just* apologized and you're *still* jealous. I thought someone who's constantly harping about being fair and looking at all angles of a story would at least try to see this one from mine."

"Wait!" I said again, but Gordon stepped onto his skateboard and pushed out of the barn.

Gloria sighed. "Look, this has been fun and all, but I know Dr. Burke. She doesn't back down. If she's out to end the paper, it's toast. Besides, between that, work building up at the diner, and school starting soon, maybe we should take a break."

"We can't take a break," I said. "The news doesn't stop!"

But Gloria strode out of the barn, patting Woodward on the head as she left.

"Who's going to cover the news if *we* don't?" I whispered.

"In case you haven't noticed, we *are* the news," Min said. "That's kind of the problem."

———————

Down to just the four of us—Thom, Woodward, Stuff, and me—I checked my phone to read the email from the AP. There it was, just as Min had said. The reporter wrote that she wanted to focus on "the lack of actual press in the area and the gap being filled not by journalists but by children working out of a barn." I quickly drafted a response highlighting her **inherent bias**.

"What does that mean?" Thom asked. I hadn't realized he was reading over my shoulder.

"It means that she already believes we aren't capable of doing a good job before she's even interviewed us or read our paper," I said. "Bias means believing something to be right or wrong without checking it out first."

"Oh," Thom said. "Sort of like how you think print journalism is more important than photojournalism."

I gasped. "I most certainly do *not*!"

Thom shrugged. "You called Gordon's photo silly and lucky. Would you say the same thing if *you* had been on the scene? If it had been your story that was breaking news?"

"That . . . that is not fair."

Thom sat down next to Stuff. Both of them tilted their heads at me. Stuff grumbled deep in his throat.

"I have to go," I said.

———————

With Woodward in my arms, I walked to the park and went straight for the swings.

Before, when we lived in the city, Dad and I would go to the city park by our apartment every single day. He would push me on the swing until I went so high I'd bounce in the seat and land with a *plop* back onto the plastic. Sometimes, the whole metal swing set would bop into the air an inch or so. We'd talk the whole time, even though sometimes I'd only catch half of every sentence (just the part when I'd sail by him). A lot of the time, I'd talk about myself, about whatever I was researching that week.

I used to research a lot. Like I'd think about something I was curious about and Mom would take me to the library, or we'd go to a museum, or I'd just sit and think about it until I had a notebook full of ideas. It could be anything—dinosaurs, electricity, DNA and hereditary principles. Dad would ask with whom I had shared my research or if I had run into any friends while working, but I would usually pretend that I was swinging too far away to have properly heard the questions.

Since Dad's been gone, most of the time I sit and think is focused on him. On what he *would* be saying or what he had said at other times. I'm pretty sure I know why he took me to the park every day. I don't think it was because he wanted it to be a special moment between just the two of us. Maybe he wanted me to find someone else at the park, like a friend. And maybe that's why Mom and Dad always were excited when I wanted to research stuff. Maybe they thought in the middle of scouring the natural history museum, I'd bump into someone my size also pursuing a research project and make a connection.

Meeting friends always has been tough. Keeping them seemed impossible. Mom said it was because although my brain capacity was greater than that of most people my age, my emotional state was exactly age appropriate.

One time, when Dad and I were leaving our apartment, Alejandro stepped out of his across the hall. "Hey!" Dad said, his voice too loud and cheerful. "We're going to the park and then to get some cones. Want to join us?"

Alejandro's mouth had twitched when Dad mentioned ice cream. "I was heading to the park anyway," he said. Dad had whooped and soon the three of us were walking together. Even worse? When we got there, Alejandro sat on the swings next to me.

For an hour, Dad asked him question after question. I learned that Alejandro likes the color orange, that his dad thought he should play baseball, and that he thinks Bubble

Yum is overrated. Then Dad stopped asking questions and looked at me. He wiggled his eyebrows and said he'd go see about those ice cream cones.

Alejandro stared at me. I stared back. *Think,* I ordered my brain. Gum! I knew a lot about gum, thanks to the five-page research paper I had written on it just for fun earlier that summer. So, I started telling him about gum, mostly reciting what I had written from memory. Dad came back, saw me talking—me telling Alejandro that the first gum sold in America was made out of chalk and charcoal. Alejandro ate his cone so fast he got a headache, which made me laugh. So that he'd have some helpful information in the future, I told him it was just his blood vessels contracting.

Later in our apartment, Dad said, "You did it, Nellie! I think you really made a friend today. All you had to do was put yourself out there."

But when I went out on the balcony that night to work on blowing bubbles, thinking maybe I'd show it to Alejandro the next time we went to the park, he was on the sidewalk below me talking to his mom. "*Why* do I have to hang out with her?" he whined. "There's a reason she's lonely. She's boring. I don't think she even knows how to have fun."

I dragged my feet through the dirt at Bear Creek Park now, holding Woodward and thinking about that moment. It's odd, isn't it, how when a person is feeling sad her brain will do everything it can to dredge up all the other times she's felt that way.

CHAPTER ELEVEN

"HEY," SOMEONE SAID BEHIND me.

I turned in the swing, crunching the metal chains together to see Gloria standing there. "Hey! I thought you had to work."

Gloria slumped into the swing beside me. She didn't push off, though, just pivoted in little circles and sighed. "Yeah, well, turns out I don't know anything."

I didn't have a response to that, so I just said, "Oh."

She twisted slowly back and forth, and I realized her eyes were wet. A big part of me wanted to get up off the swings and run home. I don't like to see other people's sadness, especially when my own pulsed against my skin. Woodward shifted in my arms. "Here." I plopped the kitten onto her lap.

"Why?" she said as she held Woodward up to look into her green eyes. She pulled her close and cuddled her against her neck. Gloria's angry twists in the swing softened.

"You just looked like you needed to hold a kitten," I said, my cheeks flaming. Gloria nodded, her shoulders rising and falling in a quiet cry. "Do you want to talk about it?"

"You wouldn't understand," she mumbled, dragging her heels in the dirt.

I straightened my back. "I might. I'm eleven and three-quarters."

Gloria paused. Both she and Woodward looked at me. "So . . . you're one of *those* kids."

"What kids?"

"The ones who add quarters to their age. You're eleven. Be eleven."

Fact: I was eleven and seven-twelfths.

"Biologically, I am eleven," I conceded. "But I have a superior intellect."

This time Woodward sighed. Gloria giggled.

"It's my dad," she said softly, just when I was trying to figure out how to get my cat back and go home. "He wasn't interviewing that woman to be a waitress."

"Isn't that a good thing? I thought you didn't want him to hire another worker."

Gloria put Woodward on her lap and rubbed the kitten right behind her velvet ears. "Yeah, *that* part is good. But they've been talking a lot because they're . . . dating."

"Oh." And then, because my brain suddenly felt like mush, it just made the same sound again, only a little softer. A thousand nosey questions burst to the surface. I knew from overhearing Gloria talk with Chef Wells that her mother had left Bear Creek months before Mom and I had moved to town, but I didn't know why. If I had been interviewing Gloria for an article, I would've asked all of the questions— has he dated anyone before? Where is your mother? When did she leave? Is she going to come back?—but Gloria wasn't sitting beside me because she was a source for an article; she was my friend. And I wasn't as great at being a friend as I was at being a reporter, but I was pretty sure if she wanted me to know the answers to those questions, she'd share them without me prompting.

"It's not a big deal." Gloria looked down at Woodward instead of me. "I want him to be happy, right? And I know Mom's not coming back. It's just . . ."

"Confusing?"

"Yeah." She buried her face in Woodward's side.

I swallowed a lump of don't-want-to-talk-about-it pain. "When my dad died," I said, and the lump grew talons and started to claw back up my throat. I swallowed again. "I felt a lot all at once. But you know what?" The lump's jagged edges made my voice sharper than maybe it should've been. "Parents *aren't supposed to leave.* So, when they do, there isn't a right way to feel. Which means there isn't a *wrong* way, either. However you feel, however long you feel it, is okay."

Gloria softly turned in her swing seat. "You know," she said at last, "you're pretty smart."

"Fact."

She stood and pressed Woodward against her neck one more time before handing the kitten over to me. "If only you were smart enough to fix this Newspaper Club."

And suddenly the lump wedged right back in my throat.

I sat for a long time thinking after Gloria headed back to the diner.

I had messed up my friendship with Gordon and maybe even with the rest of the Newspaper Club. And Thom was right that a lot of that came down to bias—I thought I knew more than them, which meant I should be in charge. I *did* know more—after all I had been in journalism my whole life—but that *didn't* mean I should be in charge of everything. And it didn't mean that the rest of the staff's work was less important than what I did.

But here was another fact: Bear Creek deserved a newspaper. And I needed friends. I wasn't about to lose either, despite what Dr. Burke said. *Atta girl, Nellie,* I heard in my dad's voice, or maybe it was Chief Rodgers's, as I pushed off the swing.

The Newspaper Club wasn't the only thing on my mind, though. I also had to respond to the AP reporter and to convince Mom that we needed Woodward in our lives. Priority one was Woodward. Already the kitten had saved me from two awkward friend conversations. Plus, when she purred against me, I felt safe.

But Mom wouldn't commit to keeping her without getting her checked out and making sure she didn't already belong to someone else. So in the morning, we went to Bear Creek Veterinary Clinic with Woodward, who, it turned out, was not a big fan of riding in the car.

"I didn't think a cat could howl like that," Mom muttered, rubbing her temples as we got out of the car. Thom's Ma let us borrow a pet carrier. It was brown with slots for Woodward to breathe through, but my favorite part was the thick handle on the top. I was tempted to swing it like Dad used to swing his briefcase beside him as he walked, but of course I didn't do that because I'm a responsible pet owner.

"Listen, we're just getting her checked out," Mom said, and I mouthed along as she said, "Pets are a lot of work."

She had repeated that sentence all morning. Woodward had slept in the carrier beside my bed, mewing most of the night. I knew she really wanted to be in my bed with me, but I had promised Mom I wouldn't let her until the vet made sure she was sickness-free.

Mom grabbed my shoulders and locked me in place with her eyes. "Listen, Nellie. We've been through a lot. I'm just beginning to feel like I'm okay, that you're okay. If Woodward is sick or too much responsibility or belongs to someone else, I don't want to go through another loss. I can't."

I cradled the carrier against my chest. "I can't, either." I lifted my chin.

Once inside, the vet held Woodward in one hand as she examined her little body. "I'd say you have an excellent friend here." The vet handed Woodward back to me.

"How do we know she doesn't belong to anyone else?" Mom asked.

The vet told her that feral, or wild, cats often roam the area. People who haven't spayed or neutered their cats sometimes dump the kittens in more rural areas like along Morgan Road. "It's tragic. Few of the kittens stand a chance. You have a fighter here."

We left the clinic with medicine (you do not want to know what the medicine treated, believe me). Then we went to the pet store for kitten food, a collar, and toys.

I held Woodward as we checked out litter boxes. "Listen," I whispered, my mouth a couple inches from her little gray head, "I'm not sure how you're supposed to learn how to use this, but do it fast, okay?" Woodward mewed.

Mom picked out a pink sparkly collar. "So people will know she's a girl."

"She's a cat. *She* doesn't know she's a girl." I replaced the collar with a nice sensible black one. "Black goes with everything."

"Fair point." Mom slid her credit card into a machine to engrave a little metal tag with Woodward's name and our phone number underneath it. I held it in my hand, still warm, when the machine spit it out. WOODWARD MURROW. Fact: This made it official. She was ours.

I grabbed a black harness and leash, too.

"Cats don't normally enjoy going for walks," Mom observed.

"Woodward isn't an ordinary cat. She's a newspaper cat." Sure enough, when I attached the harness and leash, Woodward pranced beside me toward the register. Of course, it might be because my shoelace was untied, and she had a thing for shoelaces.

At the checkout line, I paused in front of a bulletin board to scan for potential news leads. Maybe if we had a super-solid news cycle for the next issue, people would focus on *that* and not on us. But, instead, I spotted a flyer for the school board meeting. I didn't realize Mom was right behind me. "Is it usual to put up ads for a school board meeting?" she mused, and then said, "Ah" as she ran her finger across an item along the bottom of the sheet. *Also on the agenda is discussion on appropriateness of local kids' clubs and initiation of school-sponsored, supervised alternatives.*

I growled so loud the dog in line behind me joined in.

CHAPTER TWELVE

WITH THE NEWSPAPER CLUB problems and a new cat, I hadn't had any time to worry about school starting. This was strange because worrying about school starting usually preoccupied my mind from mid-July through what remained of summer. Also, this was going to be my first year attending Bear Creek Intermediate, which was for students in fourth through sixth grade. So, I should have been extra preoccupied with back-to-school stress.

I should have been making lists of social anxieties and strategies for dealing with group projects (the key was to join forces with another nerd immediately) plus inventorying my school supplies and cross-checking with the required-items list. By August, my backpack should have been loaded with blank notebooks, sharpened pencils, and various sizes and colors of sticky notes. Yet here I was, a week away from school beginning, and I hadn't even unpacked last year's workbooks from my backpack.

Something fluttered through me at the thought of last school year. In the weeks and months following when we lost Dad, all of my teachers had told me to take my time and that turning in assignments was optional (I guess they thought that I carried too much grief to remember schoolwork). But school had been a release from the bricks of sadness that seemed to block Mom and me in thick corrals whenever we were in our apartment. I actually ended up doing more schoolwork than ever.

But now? I didn't want to open my old backpack. Mom had unpacked it from one of the boxes that still lined our stairway and had it hanging from a doorknob in the kitchen. She caught me staring at it while I finished my breakfast. "I downloaded the supply list from the school website," Mom said, then blew on the top of her coffee, sending the steam toward me like well wishes. "We could go to the office store this afternoon."

"Do you think you could pick up everything without me?" I looked down at my plate. "And maybe a new backpack, too?"

Mom didn't say anything for a long time. "Yeah, I can do that. Something with rainbows and kittens, right?"

"Just black!" Woodward hopped up and curled into a ball on my lap. "But maybe a kitten keychain?"

Mom whistled low. "Way to be wild, Nellie."

Mom dropped me off at the Bear Creek Land Trust on the way to run errands.

"Is that a cat?" the lady behind the counter asked as I approached.

"Yes." That out of the way, I lowered Woodward to the ground. She was on the harness and leash so couldn't really wander too far. She attacked my shoelaces in protest. Before the lady could ask another question, I introduced myself: "My name is Nellie Murrow, and I'm a reporter for *The Cub Report*. I'm working on an article about the preserved Wilkonson land. Would you be able to help us with that or should we talk to someone else?"

"You and the cat?" the lady asked.

"Yes."

She looked at Woodward, who yawned back at her. The woman was about Ms. Wilkonson's age, with light brown skin and curly dark hair. She wore a polo with the land trust's logo of two trees and a moose. Her name tag said *Sally San Miguel*. I scribbled all of this into my notebook. If this were a breaking news story, I might not have noted much more than her name, but because I was working on a feature, I might be able to add more details into the story.

Ms. San Miguel shrugged, then showed me a map of Bear Creek that marked off the land trust areas, including Ms. Wilkonson's area.

"What is it called?" I pointed to the largest parcel.

Ms. San Miguel smiled. "Well, it just so happens that Patty Wilkonson asked us to rename it." I bounced on my toes, pen at the ready. Having a news angle would make the feature even stronger.

"Right now," Ms. San Miguel continued, "it's called Wilkonson Land Preserve. But she recently asked if we could rename it the Charlotte Land Trust."

———

Our weekly staff meeting was supposed to be that afternoon, but after yesterday's meeting I wasn't sure if we even had a staff left for a meeting. I sent out a picture of Woodward in her new collar with a group text reminder. For a long time, no one responded, but then my phone pinged with a message from Thom. *Let's meet at the creamery and have ice cream, too.*

Thom, though not a genius in the technical sense like me, had his moments. Suddenly, I had a flurry of thumbs-ups on my phone. Even Gordon liked Thom's message.

Before I left early for the meeting, I called Ms. Wilkonson to see if I could arrange a follow-up interview. She didn't answer the phone, so I left a voicemail.

I wasn't exactly sure how Miss Juliet would feel about having a cat in her shop, but thankfully the mid-August afternoon had a nice breeze, so we could sit outside. I put down my bag on the bistro table outside of the shop, looping Woodward's leash to the metal table leg, and went in to make my selection.

Miss Juliet smiled as I entered. "How are you, Nellie?"

"Okay, I guess." But I wasn't. What if everyone came thinking it would be the last Newspaper Club meeting? I was worried some of the members would *want* to be in a school-sponsored club instead of our independent press. I had an idea, but the only way it would work is if everyone in the club was in agreement.

Miss Juliet, who made all of the ice creams herself, didn't rush me as I thought about all of this while looking at the selections.

"Lonesome Lavender," I finally said.

"Are you sure?" Miss Juliet used to sell only ice creams with happy names—Resplendent Raspberry, Cheery Cheesecake, and Joyful Orangesicle were some of the options today.

"I'm sure."

Miss Juliet nodded. "Maybe your cat out there would like to try Contented Cream? I just mixed up a batch. It's still a little soft, so it would be perfect for her." I nodded. "I'm going to add a little to your scoop, too," she said. "Looks like you could use it."

Woodward and I were finishing our ice creams when Thom and Min arrived.

"I knew you'd be here early," Thom said as Min dropped her backpack on a seat.

"Because I've got so much to figure out?"

Thom shook his head. "No, because I saw when you left."

"Why didn't you ask us to come with you?" Min crossed her arms.

"We wanted to be alone." I looked down at Woodward.

Min's face scrunched together. "If you think that cat is going to replace me as your very best friend in the whole world, you. Are. Wrong." Woodward rubbed against Min's ankles, and her face smoothed out. "She *is* kind of cute. Do you think your doll clothes will fit her?"

Woodward mewed, and we both laughed. "Don't worry," I whispered to the cat. "I wouldn't do that to you."

I watched through the window as Thom and Min made their selections. I just knew they'd pick Contented Cream. I doubted they worried about anything ever.

But when Thom came back, he held a cone of Serendipitous Sherbet. "You said you had a lot to think about. What are you trying to figure out?"

I peeked through the window. Min held five sample spoons in her hand and was deep in conversation with Miss Juliet.

I wiped Lonesome Lavender from the corners of my mouth. "How the biggest news story is about *us* even though we're the ones who are supposed to be covering the news. How to make sure we cover it well. How to make sure the school board values an independent press in Bear Creek. How to fix the mess I've made with Gordon."

"That's a lot."

I didn't know Thom super well yet, but what I did know was that I couldn't predict what he'd say or do at any time. Maybe he'd share incredible advice. Maybe he'd hand me a bag of smells. Maybe he'd just sit and eat his sherbet.

Soon Gordon, Charlotte, and Gloria arrived, all of them coming from the diner to the shop. Gordon walked by me without saying hi, but he did bend to pet Woodward on top of the head.

Once he had his ice cream, Gordon picked a seat under the shade of the creamery's awning. "I'm sorry," I told him, forgetting all of my prepared speech. "I shouldn't have said your photo was lucky—and especially not silly."

"Yeah, you shouldn't have. It was mean." Gordon shrugged. "But I forgive you."

"Does your mom know you're here?"

He smirked. "She would've said no way to meeting at Thom's house, but I told her I was getting ice cream with friends."

Thom and Charlotte pulled over another bistro table so all of us could sit together. It was nearly twilight in Bear Creek, and that meant no one was around in the sleepy little downtown.

"Listen," Gordon said to the group, "my mom tries to control everything I do. I shouldn't have joined the newspaper because I knew she'd do something like this. Like when I started playing kickball in third grade, you know, just with some guys at the park? She ended up organizing a community kickball league. And suddenly we had a schedule and uniforms and grown-ups telling us what to do." He crumpled a napkin after wiping his mouth and sat back in his chair. "She says it's to protect me, but I hate it." He took a breath. "I'll quit, okay? She'll probably back down if I quit."

"Don't say that!" I snapped. "We need you. No one's quitting." I glanced around the table. "I mean, unless you want to. We *could*, you know, make this a school thing. Thom, I know you're homeschooled, but you could still be in a school club, right?"

Something squished inside my chest as everyone around the table shook their heads. "No way," Gloria said.

"We need to be interdependent," Thom said.

"You mean *independent*," I said.

Thom didn't correct himself.

"I'm not quitting," Charlotte said, her voice uncharacteristically loud.

Min squirmed in her seat. "Mom says she wants this to be my last meeting until the club is supervised. But Dad says he likes my spunk. So, I don't know."

I pressed my lips together. Maybe Mom could talk to Mrs. Kim-Franklin and help her see that our newspaper was safe for Min. "Well," I said, "first agenda item is resolved: we're keeping the paper. Now we have to figure out the next issue. First off, I think the biggest story is the school board's efforts to push out *The Cub Report* and to make a school-sponsored newspaper."

"It's more than that," Gordon said. "It's about whether we're capable of doing a newspaper."

"Whether we *should,*" Charlotte amended. "That's the allusion made in the *Burlington Meadows* column."

I nodded and winked at Charlotte for using a form of the word **allude,** which means something hinted at in a text. Her forehead wrinkled and she looked behind her. I'd have to work on subtle gestures for showing approval for her great grammar. "Yes, all of those issues. Our top story should be the school board's efforts to end or change *The Cub Report.* Secondary issues could be the impact of Gordon's photograph and the national attention it received, along with the response to us having a newspaper."

"Wait!" Min held up her hand like a stop sign. "This goes against everything you've been saying. Just last week, you were a complete bossy pants about how we can't cover ourselves in our newspaper. Now you're saying practically the whole issue is going to be *The Cub Report* itself?"

I let the bossy pants jab slide and nodded. "I don't like it, but that's the news right now."

"Okay," Gloria said and looked up from where she was taking notes. "So, Nellie's going to cover the school board meeting—"

"No," I interrupted. "I can't cover it. I'm going to speak at the meeting, so I can't cover the story."

"Wait! What?" Gordon said.

I straightened my back. "I'm going to talk at the meeting. I'm going to invite the AP reporter to be there, too." Then I remembered the bossy pants comment and added, "If that's okay with all of you."

Thom suggested that Gloria cover the school board meeting. Gordon would take photographs.

"Also," I said to Gordon, "I think you should write a column about taking that image of the convict. Maybe you could reference the national coverage it has received?"

"Wait, I'd be writing the lead story?" Gloria smiled. "Do you think I'm ready for this?"

"Absolutely. The way you handled the town's responses in the last issue was fantastic." Gloria and I fist-bumped. "The only issue might be keeping coverage as unbiased as possible."

Gloria rolled her eyes. "Miss Marcia, the old receptionist for the *Gazette,* was at the diner for the meatloaf special last week, and I listened to her talk for an hour straight about how she does nothing but work, work, work for everyone even though she should be retired, and not once did I interrupt her to point out that she'd get a whole lot more done if she didn't brag about herself so much. I've got this."

Thom was watching my face. I think I knew why—it wasn't like me to give up the lead story. But maybe it should be.

Charlotte sidled closer to me. "What are you going to write about for this issue?"

"I think I should write an editorial about the importance of an independent press." I looked at her. "Plus, I'd like to write a feature about Ms. Wilkonson's land trust." Her cheeks flushed, and that confirmed a hunch—I knew it wasn't random that she had picked that intersection on the Bear Creek map and suggested I go there for a story. "Maybe you could read over what I've written so far?" I pulled a folded-up sheet of printed paper from my backpack and handed it to Charlotte. It was all about Ms. Wilkonson's gardens, her land trust, and the way it uprooted her family. Charlotte held it so her face was covered as she read.

I turned to Thom. "I know you've usually done the features. This time, do you think you could do something different? The Bear Creek vet said people dump pets by the roadside; maybe you could do a story about ways to combat that?"

Min leaned forward. "I could create a map or a graphic to go with it."

"That will leave a lot of copy editing to Charlotte." I turned to her again. She had finished reading the story and now stared ahead. Everyone else continued discussing ideas, so a quiet bubble was between us. I pointed to the paper. "The story isn't finished. There's a whole side that's missing."

She stared at the paper. "I wouldn't be able to edit it, anyway. It wouldn't be okay to edit a story about my grandma."

CHAPTER THIRTEEN

CHARLOTTE'S FACE FLAMED BRIGHT red. "I should've told you," she said. "I thought you wouldn't cover the story if you knew it was about my grandma, even though I've never even met her."

I pressed together my lips. "It wasn't right to trick me like that. I think I *would've* said no to that article a week ago. And I *do* think the newspaper shouldn't try to be part of the story. But sometimes, like now, it is. We all live in Bear Creek, and Bear Creek is so small—I've come to realize that occasionally we're going to be part of the stories we share."

Charlotte glanced around the table. The rest of the club was busy talking to each other and not paying attention to us. "I wouldn't have been able to tell you much, anyway. Mom never wants to talk about her. She says that she's selfish and would rather have her trees than her family."

"I don't think she's like that at all." I squirmed in my seat, thinking about how the land was about to be renamed after a granddaughter Ms. Wilkonson had never met. "Do you think maybe you could go with me tomorrow? To talk to her?"

Charlotte shook her head. Her bottom lip quivered and tears pooled in her big green eyes.

Quickly, I scooped up Woodward from under my seat and deposited her on Charlotte's lap. Woodward curled into a semi-circle. "I only know where she lives because I overheard Mom and Granddad fighting. Granddad said enough time has passed and maybe he had been hotheaded and wrong about things." Charlotte's fingers made rivulets in the kitten's fur. "He said I should meet her. He said maybe she was lonely. Maybe she had a hard time saying how she feels because her feelings go so deep inside it's hard to make the words come out. Maybe she seems like she doesn't care, but really she's caring way too much. Maybe she's just like—" Charlotte shuddered.

"Like what?"

"Like me," she whispered. Her shoulders shook and tears fell on Woodward's back.

Thom nudged my side. The rest of the club kept on talking to each other, but they each glanced at me. Gordon tilted his head toward Charlotte and his eyebrow popped up. Gloria mouthed my name. Min mimed putting her arm out around someone. *Oh.* I reached my arm around Charlotte's shaking shoulders. It felt super awkward, and I *had* already given her a kitten to hold—but I knew it was the right thing to do when Charlotte took a shaky breath and leaned back into my arm.

I wasn't sure how long I had to leave my arm there or when it would begin to lose circulation, but I was glad it being there seemed to help Charlotte. She wiped her cheeks with her hands, then lifted Woodward to her face. Slowly, just in case it wasn't time, I brought my arm back to my lap. Min caught my eye and nodded. *Good job,* she mouthed.

Soon, Gordon left, telling us he'd have a column about the viral photograph ready for copy editing soon. "I'm not talking to my mom but spending all day in my room, so it shouldn't take too long." I thought about handing over Woodward again after that, but Charlotte still held her.

Gloria left shortly after. She wanted to make sure her dad didn't need help closing the diner. Mr. Kim-Franklin pulled up in his car just then to take Min home. He offered me and Thom a ride too, but Min reminded him that Mrs. Kim-Franklin was allergic to cats. "I'm sure she won't notice," he said, but Thom told him his moms would be there soon.

"They're just picking up a few things across the street," he said. My forehead wrinkled. The store Thom had pointed to only sold baby stuff. It would be odd for Thom to lie. Maybe Stuff needed diapers? I hadn't ever seen the goat in diapers, but I didn't know a lot about goats.

Charlotte called her parents to make sure it was okay if Thom's parents gave her a ride home, and I texted Mom to let her know we'd be home soon. "I can walk," I told Thom, lifting up Woodward. "She cries a lot in the car."

"That's okay," he said. "The baby cries in the car a lot, too."

"The baby? You got that baby goat your ma wanted?" Woodward batted my cheek to calm me down.

Thom didn't answer, just pointed across the street where Sheila, his ma, walked out of the shop with armloads of bags. She held open the door for Melanie, his mom, who pushed a stroller through the doorway. Inside the stroller was not a goat.

It was a human baby.

———

As an only child, I hadn't been around a lot of babies. This one looked to be maybe a year old—like a toddler—based on the length of her wavy, dark hair. She had big brown eyes and a dimple that deepened when she caught a glimpse of Thom. In fact, her whole body reacted to seeing him, her arms shaking and legs kicking. She was trying hard to say something to him, but it came out as *blurga-blub-bub*.

"You have a baby!" I said. "When did this happen?"

Thom shrugged. "About a week ago."

Charlotte whistled. "And everyone says *I'm* quiet."

Thom shoved his hands in his pockets. "She's not ours forever. I mean, she might not be." He swung his foot around the table leg. "We're taking care of her—her parents aren't able to—but if they do become able, they'll take her back."

His moms were now in front of us. The baby gurgled and pumped her fists. "Hey!" Sheila said. "Meet Josephina. We've been calling her Josie."

"Look." Melanie pointed to Woodward, who went up on her back legs to peek at the baby. "It's Josie and the Pussycat." I wasn't sure what that meant, but it made Thom's moms laugh.

Charlotte leaned into the baby, taking her fist and introducing herself with a handshake. Josie giggled, but her eyes stayed on Thom. Finally, he brushed a piece of her long hair away from her cheek, and she did that whole body-trying-to-say-something wiggle and gurgle again.

"She just loves Thom," Sheila said.

We walked down the street to where Thom's parents' minivan was parked. Charlotte kept up with Josie, still holding her little hand as Sheila pushed the stroller.

"I've always wanted a little sister," Charlotte said.

Thom sighed beside me.

"Are you okay?" I started to hand over Woodward, but he laughed. Not his usual quiet, shiny-eyes laugh, either. This one was brittle.

"I don't need to hold the cat."

"Don't you like Josie?"

Thom's head jerked toward me. "Of course I like her. She's awesome!" He looked forward again, while some of Josie's giggles trickled back to us. "But it's going to hurt when she goes back. My moms have been foster parents before. The last one was a boy about our age. He stayed with us for three months. Now, I don't know where he is."

"So, you're trying not to love her?"

Thom didn't answer, and we walked silently to the car. The minivan had two captain chairs in the middle and a bench in the way back. Josie's car seat snapped into a harness in a captain seat, and Charlotte sat in the one beside her. Thom, Woodward, and I crawled back to the bench seat. Woodward didn't howl so long as I held her close to my chest. I was positioning her into place when Charlotte held up a book she had plucked from the ground between the seats.

It was large, like the size of a textbook, with a white nubbly-looking cover. On it was a golden fairy. "Is this yours?" Charlotte asked Thom.

"No," Thom said. "It's Josie's."

I laughed, thinking he was joking. What was a baby doing with a big book like that? It looked super old. But Thom just shrugged. "The social worker said her last foster sister gave it to her."

Thom took it from Charlotte and flipped to the cover page. A child's careful signature was at the top: *Stephanie Matthews.*

Underneath it were two more names written in a different child's handwriting. *Kit and Caleb,* and a sketch of two trees. *Josie, this book is yours now. Don't forget me. ~Kit.*

I read the writing out loud. Thom looked out the window. "She's just a baby. She won't remember any of us."

I studied the words. "Maybe."

Thom snorted.

I shrugged. "I mean, yeah, she won't remember Kit, but she'll have these stories, I guess."

Thom handed the book back to Charlotte, who ran her thumb over the penciled sketch of the trees. Sheila pulled to a stop in front of Charlotte's sprawling brick house. A big crystal chandelier sparkled in the foyer window. The hedge around the house was tidy and perfectly squared. The yard had two symmetrical trees, each with a spotlight under them. I had a flash of Ms. Wilkonson's wild gardens.

Charlotte hopped out and then, realizing she still held Josie's book, leaned back in. "I'm going to go with you tomorrow," she said in her careful, quiet way. "I should meet her."

"Okay, but I already have a couple moms upset with me."

"I'll tell my mom I'm going with you." Charlotte's face was stern.

For the rest of the drive home, Sheila and Melanie talked about diapers, pureed food, and nighttime routines. Thom and I didn't talk at all. Josie kicked, giggled, and clapped.

"She's really cute," I said. "You know, for a baby."

Thom nodded.

We passed Bear Creek Park. The moonlight seemed to shine on the empty swing set. A crow perched on the crossbar.

I glanced over at Thom; he was making a face at Josie, sticking his tongue out and crossing his eyes. Josie giggled. When he noticed me looking at him, he quickly glanced away. I nudged his side. "Gordon said something to me when we were working on that story about the crows. He said the birds let themselves feel sad."

Thom didn't say anything. I nudged him again. "I think it's going to hurt no matter what if she leaves. But she's here now."

Thom's eyes snagged on Josie's and she wiggled again. He nodded and tickled her foot. "That's true."

CHAPTER FOURTEEN

CHARLOTTE WAS AT MY house at ten o'clock the next morning. She wore cut-off shorts and a plain blue T-shirt and had a notebook and pens tucked in her back pocket. An older man had dropped her off. "Was that your grandpa?" I asked her.

Charlotte nodded. I waited for her to say something more, but she didn't.

"Did you tell your mom?"

She nodded again.

We looked at each other for another minute.

"Okay. Let's go."

Min had said Charlotte could borrow her bike for the day so long as I left Woodward behind for her to cat-sit. I glanced toward Min's house; she made Woodward wave to me from an upstairs window. That Min was always watching.

Charlotte's eyes widened at Min's bike with its pink streamers and white basket. Charlotte would never dot an *i* with a heart. She cringed when I handed her the bright pink bicycle helmet, but she strapped it on.

I thought maybe Charlotte would start talking as we pedaled up Morgan Road, but she was completely silent. Her face was a little red, which might've been from taking on the hill. After a few minutes, I said, "Ms. Wilkonson's really nice. I mean, mostly nice."

Charlotte sort of nodded. "Grandpa's really nice."

"Oh, yeah?" I prompted.

But she didn't say anything for another fifteen minutes, until we reached the end of Ms. Wilkonson's stone driveway. Then she stepped off Min's bike and laid it on the grass. "I gave Mom your story. She said it left out a lot."

I laid my bike next to hers. "It's just a first draft."

Charlotte rolled her eyes. "That's not what she meant. But she said if I wanted to meet her mother, it was up to me. She said she needs more time before seeing her."

We walked down the driveway, striding close enough to each other that our shoulders brushed. As we approached the porch, the floorboards squeaked and the screen door flew open. "Oh," I said, "I probably should've mentioned—Ms. Wilkonson and I didn't leave on really great terms."

Ms. Wilkonson stormed down her front steps. "I told you, I don't think I want—"

Then she saw Charlotte standing beside me. Her hands flew to her mouth.

"Hi . . ." Charlotte's mouth changed shape like it was planning to speak more words. *Grandma,* maybe. Or *Ms. Wilkonson.* She pressed her lips together.

"Charlotte." Ms. Wilkonson pulled her hands from her mouth. One hand sort of drifted toward us, then fell to her side. "You look just like Susie when she was your age."

I wished I had brought Woodward along. I think both of them could've used a kitten right about then.

———————

Ms. Wilkonson brought out cookies and lemonade, and we sat in the garden. I noticed the cookies had chocolate chips.

She asked Charlotte a lot of questions—what she liked to do ("read"), whether she played sports ("not really"), if she liked school ("mostly"), but neither of them seemed to know how to be around each other. They both jumped when the other spoke. As for me, I pretended to be a lump. Finally, Ms. Wilkonson asked if we wanted to go for a walk. "I could show you Charlotte Land Trust."

Ms. Wilkonson squirted peppermint oil on our arms and legs to ward off ticks and bugs, then we headed down the little trail into the woods. We paused at the clearing. Charlotte stood in the middle and spun around. "Do all trees take so long to grow back? It's so quiet in this empty patch."

Ms. Wilkonson paused. "It depends on the forest. Rainforests wouldn't be the same for, by some estimates, decades or even thousands of years. The interesting thing to me, though, is work by a scientist who showed that even a few downed trees can affect the sounds in a forest. Nearly thirty years after selective deforestation—where only a few trees are cut down rather than a whole patch like this—the number of animal sounds and birdsong in a forest aren't recovered."

Charlotte brushed the tops of the ferns with her hands. "It's like an interrupted story." She looked at me. "Like what you said would happen when the *Gazette* closed, the reason we needed to write our own newspaper, so the stories wouldn't stop."

Ms. Wilkonson gestured for Charlotte to follow her. "Charlotte Land Trust isn't like this open plot of land," she said. "It's a full forest, just a little farther down the trail. Yesterday I saw a family of river otters playing in the stream there."

Charlotte grinned and trotted ahead. "Are you coming?" she asked me at the clearing's edge.

I shook my head and pulled out my notebook from my back pocket. "I think I'm going to go sit in the garden. I want to work on my editorial."

"But don't you want to cover this for your story?"

I glanced at Ms. Wilkonson, noticing how she and Charlotte had the same smile. "No, I think I've got everything I need."

Sometimes it was hard to hear Dad's voice when I thought about the things he taught me. But just then? I heard him as clearly as if he were still beside me. In the memory, I had visited him in the newsroom. He had gone into a small conference room with a reporter. The reporter was first to leave the room. Her mouth was set in a firm line and her hands were in fists. She didn't go back to her cubicle; she went straight to the ladies' room and slammed the door. Dad left the conference room with his hand combing back his hair and his eyes on the ground.

"Are you okay?" I had asked him.

Dad nodded. "Being news editor sometimes means stopping a story. This was a story that didn't need to be told, one that didn't serve our readers, and she wasn't happy to hear it." Here's the part that echoed in my mind as I sat in Ms. Wilkonson's lonely garden: *It's up to us to decide which stories to share, by whom and to what degree. It's a sacred responsibility. And sometimes the responsible thing to do is to say no, or even not yet.*

Just before Charlotte and her grandmother came back through the woods, I had drafted my editorial. When I saw them, it was like a stream just after a large rock had been kicked away; instead of silence there was an outpouring of laughter and storytelling happening.

"Can I come back soon?" Charlotte asked at the end of the driveway as she strapped on Min's bright pink helmet.

Ms. Wilkonson reached out and squeezed Charlotte's hand. "Please do. As soon as you can. And . . . tell your mom I . . ."

Charlotte squeezed her grandmother's hand back. "I'll tell her."

———

That evening, I lay on my stomach on the fluffy rug next to where Mom worked on her book. With the laptop in front of me, I wrote my editorial and the article about the Charlotte Land Trust. Mom handed me Twizzlers to chew on while we worked. It was funny—Dad couldn't stand quiet rooms. He had needed a nonstop flurry of activity in order to write. At home, his office always had music blasting. But Mom's attic was quiet except for the whirl of the oscillating fan in the corner and the snaps of us biting off pieces of licorice.

Woodward snoozed beside me. After I sent Gloria my editorial, I started to work on the story about Charlotte Land Trust. Soon, I sent that one to Charlotte.

The Wilkonson Land Preserve, comprising more than 90 acres in West Bear Creek, will be renamed Charlotte Land Trust, sources connected to Bear Creek Land Trust confirmed.

Patricia Wilkonson of Bear Creek donated the land, which had been in her family for generations, to the trust in the early 2000s. She recently asked the trust to rename it in honor of her granddaughter, who is a copy editor at The Cub Report.

"I had dreams that one day my daughter would have her own children, and they'd play here, too, turning fallen trees into playgrounds," Ms. Wilkonson said of why she preserved the land, which is home to birds, moose, otters, bears, deer, foxes, squirrels, and lots of ticks, as well as other animals.

Ms. Wilkonson campaigned in the early 2000s for Maine to offer tax incentives for landowners to sign over land to the trust. She keeps the pen used to sign the legislation in a velvet box in her living room but spends most of her time in her gardens and woods.

Charlotte FaceTimed me a minute later. I didn't want to disturb Mom, so I moved to the stairs to take the call. "Your story left out everything about the fight. It doesn't mention it at all."

I nodded.

I didn't want everyone at Wells Diner sitting around talking about Ms. Wilkonson and whether it was right to keep that pen boxed up in her living room and her land full of trees.

"But I wanted Mom and Grandpa to read it!" Charlotte's cheeks turned pink and her forehead wrinkled. "I wanted to make them understand!"

I thought about the first issue of *The Cub Report,* when Thom wrote about Miss Juliet and left out the sadness. She decided to share that part herself, through her ice cream flavors like Lonesome Lavender.

"Then I'll help you write it for them."

CHAPTER FIFTEEN

IN THE MORNING, GLORIA emailed me with corrections. *Wow* was her only comment. I didn't know if that was a good or a bad wow.

I had emailed the Associated Press reporter about the school board meeting. I added that members of *The Cub Report* would be available for questions following the meeting. The reporter didn't respond, so I wasn't sure if *The Cub Report* was still even news.

"You ready?" Mom asked before the school board meeting.

"Ready." I smoothed my black dress and glanced in the mirror by the door to make sure my hair looked okay. I had borrowed an orange headband from Min to cover the patches of hair missing from around my forehead. Woodward hopped onto the couch and watched me. "I'm still me, I promise."

When we walked outside, Mrs. Kim-Franklin was standing by the porch, holding Min's hand. Her eyes widened. "Wow, Nellie. You look lovely."

Of course, she did, too. She wore a red sundress with a shiny black belt and shiny black sandals. Next to her, Min wore red ruffled shorts and a black tank top. She also wore a black ruffled headband. I narrowed my eyes at it. "Yeah," Min said, "I know I told you I didn't have a black headband. You need a little color in your life."

"That's lying."

"No." Min put her hands on her hips, and I noticed that the scratches from Woodward were healing nicely. She had tried to put the cat in a tutu while Charlotte and I visited Ms. Wilkonson. "It's guiding you toward better choices."

Mom and Mrs. Kim-Franklin had been sorority sisters at Penn State, and usually they did this odd, super-giggly handshake, even if it was just when the two of them happened to be at the mailbox at the same time. But now they stood awkwardly facing each other.

"I've thought a lot about what you said about the Newspaper Club," Mrs. Kim-Franklin said to Mom, "and I'll keep an open mind."

"Thank you," Mom said. "You look beautiful, by the way."

"Thank you," Mrs. Kim-Franklin said. "You also look great." Mom was again wearing one of Dad's band T-shirts, but this one was paired with pants that had a button and a zipper. She also was wearing jewelry—a bunch of bracelets and a pair of dangly earrings. It wasn't an outfit I'd ever expect to see on Mom. I was beginning to think she'd never wear her old wardrobe again.

Mrs. Kim-Franklin looped her arm around Mom's waist. They stayed like that the whole four blocks to the school board meeting. Min lifted her arm toward me, and I shook my head. "We're not there yet." She skipped beside me instead.

I had my column mostly memorized but also printed on paper. I rubbed the paper in my hands until it felt as soft as Woodward's ears. (Mom wouldn't budge on not allowing me to bring the kitten along to the meeting, even though I felt pretty sure Dr. Burke would have a change in perspective if she held Woodward for a bit.)

We were early to the meeting, but the community center conference room was packed. "Is it usually like this?" Mom asked Mrs. Kim-Franklin.

She shook her head. "Never."

Then I noticed that about a half dozen people held reporters' notebooks. A television reporter stood next to a videographer, checking to make sure there were clear views of the podium and the microphone. My eyes narrowed when Randolph Yellow barged through the doors, holding his notebook and telling everyone to let him through. "I'm with the *Burlington Meadows Journal,* the *only* professional local press."

The school board members took seats at a U-shaped table. I recognized Miss Marcia but didn't know any other members. Then Dr. Burke took a seat. The buzz among the reporters increased as she sat down. I scanned the rest of the room. Chef Wells was in a middle row, sitting next to Gloria, who held her notebook in her hand. She had opted for a yellow steno notebook instead of a reporter's notebook, but I didn't make a face or say anything about it because I'm mature. Thom sat between his parents, with Josie on his lap. I spied a few other people I knew, including Mrs. Austin, Miss Juliet, Ms. Wilkonson, Charlotte, and her parents and grandfather. When Charlotte waved at her grandmother, her mom tilted in her seat and looked back. She didn't smile, but she *did* look. Chief Rodgers in his uniform paced the back of the room.

Gordon slid into the seat next to mine. He held up his camera and took shots of the room and his mom. Dr. Burke crossed her arms and shook her head at him, but he kept snapping pictures. "I'm going to be in so much trouble," he muttered.

Miss Marcia hit a gavel to begin the meeting. "So nice to have such a strong community support this meeting," she said in a voice that sounded a lot like it wasn't so nice. "So rare to see people actually put in the work the way I do to make this community great."

Then the board moved through the agenda. This year there would be seven kindergarten classrooms instead of the usual five, and the cafeteria budget couldn't cover new plastic trays. I made a note to check into what they would be using instead.

I was so focused on the story leads coming out of the meeting that I almost missed Dr. Burke clearing her throat. Gordon tensed beside me, and I put down my notebook.

"One last thing on the agenda tonight," Dr. Burke said. "I'd like to propose we begin a student newspaper at Bear Creek Middle School."

I gasped. While Gloria and Gordon would be entering the middle school this year as seventh graders, I was in the intermediate. That meant I wouldn't even be able to join the club! "It would be student-run with teacher guidance and supervision, making sure the participants are covering appropriate and safe topics. To facilitate it, I suggest adding a teaching position, focusing on journalism, to the budget." She looked out over the audience. "I believe this organization would better suit the needs of our community and allow for other child-led groups to disband so that members can concentrate instead on being children."

A rush of whispers erupted around the audience. Gordon groaned and Charlotte shook her head. Min curled her hands into fists.

A member of the school board leaned forward into the microphone. "I don't think we, as a school board, have the authority to disband independent community organizations." A few people—probably fellow Cubs—clapped. Gordon hooted.

"Of course," Dr. Burke said without seeming to have heard any of the murmuring. "But having a staff member dedicated to teaching journalism and running a student-organized newspaper *would* provide a safer, stronger, supported alternative. Plus, the students involved would learn from a professional news reporter, one with ties to this community."

Someone screamed *"No!"* as Randolph Yellow stepped forward and half-bowed to the audience. That someone was me.

"Hey, everyone." Randolph Yellow was wearing a loose-fitting plaid suit with a pale pink button-down shirt and brown tie. He even wore a fedora. My dad always said never to trust someone in a fedora. (This is a lie. Dad never said that. But I'm sure if he had seen Randolph Yellow, he would've said it just then.) He sauntered over to the microphone, putting his mouth right against it. "I'm a *professional* journalist. I'll teach the kids what they need to do, including when to leave stories to the pros."

Both Min and Gordon elbowed me in the sides. "Stop growling!" Gordon hissed.

Randolph Yellow took another bow, but his hat slipped from his head, so he clocked himself in the forehead with the microphone stand. He swayed a second, then scooped up the hat.

Chief Rodgers, who by then had leaned against the wall next to my row, let loose a sigh so loud from deep inside his barrel chest that it ruffled his mustache before drifting out over us.

"Yes, well," Dr. Burke said, "as I was saying, someone in the field, perhaps Mr. Yellow or someone else, could show the kids the proper way to handle reporting while also maintaining their safety in a supervised situation. Shall we vote?"

I popped up from my seat. "No!"

The school board members swiveled in their chairs to face me. I straightened my back. "I'd like to comment, please." Miss Marcia beckoned me to the microphone. I scooted out of the aisle. Min grabbed my arm and yanked me down. "Don't burp," she whispered.

"What?"

"Trust me. It'd be embarrassing." She nodded sagely, then leaned forward. "When my mom gets upset, she burps. Maybe it's because she also eats cheese when she's sad. But then all Dad and I do is laugh, which makes her angrier, which means more burps, and we're laughing too hard to hear anything but the burps. So, don't burp."

"I'm not worried about burping," I snapped. Only it was a little too loud, I guess, because suddenly people around us laughed. Even Chief Rodgers's mustache was twitching in a non-angry way. I *hadn't* been worried about burping, anyway.

I smoothed my dress and walked to the microphone. I leaned toward it, remembered Randolph Yellow, and took it from its stand to wipe it off on the edge of my dress. Then I held it up. "Nellie Murrow, news editor of *The Cub Report,* Bear Creek's only independent press."

I opened the folded-up paper with my editorial printed inside, but the words swam into each other. I didn't need it. I knew what I had to say.

"Recently, a photojournalist with *The Cub Report* was first to spot a wanted criminal who had holed up in a Bear Creek outbuilding after subsiding on petty thefts since his escape from Burlington Meadows.

"Because he is a *professional,* Gordon Burke raised his camera and snapped the images. He contacted the police and then, with fellow journalist Thom Hunter, began working the story.

"They weren't there in pursuit of a criminal. They were there to report on Annabelle Murphy, a five-year-old potbelly pig who was being blamed for the thefts and whose pen had been unknowingly taken over by the escapee." I turned to face Dr. Burke. "They were there to cover a Bear Creek story, one that could only happen here, one that involves our community and the people in it. But a larger news story found us, *and we were ready.*"

I scanned the crowd, my eyes snagging on all the familiar faces of people I knew.

"My parents, journalists Mike and Wendy Murrow, taught me that everybody has a story. More importantly, they taught me that everyone's story matters. I don't have a degree in journalism, but I do have a passion for the First Amendment, for storytelling, for facts, and for ethics. So does every member of *The Cub Report.*

"You say we need supervision—that we should be playing instead of reporting. You think *that* is what's good for us. But we're doing good for our community. We're finding out how it works and how it's rooted. And *that*'s good for all of Bear Creek. Because someday we're going to be in charge. Don't you think we should know how things work?"

A few people in the audience murmured and a couple applauded.

I looked at Ms. Wilkonson. She nodded slightly at me, and I straightened my back once more. "In researching an article for an upcoming *Cub Report* story, I learned a forest that is chopped down will recover over time. But it's disconnected. Its stories—birdsong and animal tracks—disappear.

"That's what will happen to Bear Creek if we don't find a way to share our stories. Our roots will be there, under the surface, but we won't hear the birdsong.

"Yes, I'm a kid. Yes, I might make mistakes. That's why there is a correction section in the paper. We haven't had to use it yet. *Mr.* Yellow has, when he said journalism should be reserved for professionals, not a bunch of twelve-year-olds. I'm actually eleven. Min Kim-Franklin, our graphic designer, is ten."

I gave an uncharacteristic giggle at the way people in the audience chuckled in reaction to Min's hooting and pumping fist. Quickly, I cleared my throat.

"We do have professional journalists to turn to when we need guidance, including my mom and dad. I know my dad isn't here anymore, but his stories are." This time, I looked right at Thom, who held Josie on his lap. "Stories don't go away, not if you're brave enough to share them."

I took a deep breath. *Now is not the time to get a shaky voice, Nellie Murrow,* I told myself. I glanced down at my paper. There was more written there, stuff about how our newspaper operates, how we decide what makes a news story, and who should get to cover it. But I didn't need to say anything else.

I reattached the microphone and walked back to my seat to a smattering of applause. Mom squeezed my shoulder. "I'm proud of you," she said.

I wished Woodward were there to hold, but Min slipped her hand into mine and that felt almost as nice. "Good job not burping," she whispered.

CHAPTER SIXTEEN

AFTER I SAT DOWN, Mrs. Austin stood. Her voice was quaky and frail, but the people around her shushed everyone until she could be heard. "I just want to say that no one from the *Burlington Meadows Journal* would've noticed that I needed help the way these kids from their little paper did." She smiled and gestured around the room, her hand moving out the same way it did in the park when she fed the crows. "I doubt a school paper would've noticed, either."

Chef Wells pumped his arms to move his wheelchair to the microphone. "I've got skin in the game here, due to my girl over there reporting on this meeting. But anyone who's been to Wells Diner in the past few weeks knows our menu has benefited from you all sending in recipes—recipes that were called for in *The Cub Report*. Would a school paper do that? Would the *Journal*?" A few more people cheered.

Another person stepped forward. She was about Mom's age and held a baby on her hip. "I, for one," she said, "think kids should be outside playing, not taking hardworking people's jobs."

Then I noticed Ms. Wilkonson moving slowly forward toward the podium. "I think we should give these kids a chance," she said, her voice quiet despite the microphone. "They've only had a couple of issues, right? Why not let them keep at it? I . . . I wish I had figured out how to say how I felt— what I thought about things—when I was their age." Charlotte clapped loudly as her grandmother passed them, but her mom still looked like a statue.

Miss Marcia leaned into her microphone. "Shall we vote?" The other board members nodded.

"Hold on," Dr. Burke said. "I think we should refocus and consider—"

"Stop!" Gordon got to his feet. "Just stop, Mom."

"Gordon," Dr. Burke said. "You may not speak to me this way."

"As the person who took the photograph that made this whole thing even a discussion, I think I have the right to talk, too." His voice was loud enough that everyone in the room could hear, but he was directing it only to his mom. "I know you want to keep me safe. I understand that. And I know what I did was dangerous. But I'm going to be in dangerous situations throughout my life. If I had just been skating by, I'd still be in danger. But because I had a camera, because I knew to take notes and to call the police, I stayed safe *and* I kept everyone else safe, too. And now I know that Chief Rodgers will be there in a minute flat when we need him." Chief sort of wiggled at that, at least until he saw us noticing—then he just nodded.

Dr. Burke held up a slim hand. "This is not the place to discuss this."

"No," Gordon said, "maybe it isn't. But instead of talking to me, you made a whole school board meeting out of it. I know you were scared. I was, too. I . . . I *am* still, to know that there was a criminal right in Bear Creek. That scary things can happen here. But I'd rather know because then I can prepare for what to do about it." He lifted his arms and let them fall against his sides in frustration. "You can't control everything that happens to me, Mom. You have to trust that I can handle it and be there for me when I need you."

"I *am* here for you," Dr. Burke said, her voice softer.

Randolph Yellow strode forward and stood in front of the microphone again. "Listen, okay, all of this talk about feelings and safety is great, but the truth is an independent newspaper wasn't able to hack it in this town. One run by kids doesn't have a chance. Why would you even consider having a half-rate newspaper when you could subscribe to the *Burlington Meadows Journal*, full of news from the real world?"

"The real world?" I was on my feet without even thinking. "Bear Creek has real news!"

Chief Rodgers rocked with his hands behind his back. "You know," he said, "of all the newspapers that covered that escaped convict, *The Cub Report* was the only one that reported that BCPD was on the scene in less than three minutes. The only one that interviewed the Murphys about how they're increasing security in Annabelle's pen. The only one that tied in the thefts and how they affected neighborly relations."

Thank you, I mouthed to the chief.

He nodded, pushing out his bottom lip. "This doesn't mean I like you, kid. But I dislike that guy more."

Miss Marcia tapped on her microphone. "All in favor of establishing a school-sponsored newspaper?"

The board voted against Dr. Burke's proposal, four to three. "Motion fails," she announced. "That said, should the middle school opt to create a newspaper club of its own, it will be at the principal's discretion. With that, I believe our meeting is over."

I let out a huge breath and Min leaned into my side. "We did it!"

"I'm in so much trouble," Gordon muttered as Dr. Burke left her position on the podium and moved toward us. But Dr. Burke just wrapped her arms around him in a huge, warm hug.

That night, my editorial was posted on *The Cub Report* website. It got some traction, with readers numbering a couple thousand by morning. It wasn't get-the-attention-of-*Ellen* high, but still a little bit viral. Many of the comments echoed the go-outside-and-play and kids-should-just-be-kids responses we had been receiving after Gordon's photo was published, but many more were supportive, mentioning how nice it was to read about kids helping their communities.

The morning before the first day of school, the club met in the barn to do a final edit on the latest issue. We'd print it and deliver it that afternoon. Included in that issue was a little box asking Bear Creek residents to consider donating supplies (printing paper, printer ink, reporter's notebooks, and pens) to the newspaper.

Everyone was at the barn except for Gordon. He had texted that he had to do something with his mom. I hoped he wasn't in trouble.

Min's design had the school board story as a box covering the middle of the page. The headline ran two lines: *Independent news is good news, school board decides.* The subhead said: *BCSD votes against creating school-based newspaper; town speaks in support of independent press.* Gloria's coverage of the meeting ran under the headline. My editorial ran along the far side. The photograph was me stepping away from the microphone while people in the conference room cheered. It felt strange to be the main news story. Also on the page was a blank space for Gordon's column about the unexpected response to the photograph. Thom's piece on abandoned animals included a small picture of Woodward with the caption: *A kitten left on Morgan Road was adopted by a Bear Creek resident.*

This issue included the short piece on Charlotte Land Trust and a small article on the budget information we gathered from the school board meeting.

"I liked covering the meeting," Gloria said. "It reminds me of talking with Dad about business stuff."

"Great," I said. "You're on the municipal beat from now on."

Woodward jumped off my lap and onto Thom's, angling to get closer to Stuff, who was nibbling on Thom's hair.

"Thom, since you're homeschooled, you'll be our lookout for news during the day," I said to him. "We'll keep an eye out for news in and outside of school."

"Well, we know one story already." Min bounced on her haystack.

"What's that?" Gloria asked.

"My birthday is next month! I'll be eleven, just like Nellie and Thom." Bounce, bounce, bounce.

I nearly told her I was actually eleven and two-thirds, but I was no longer one of *those* kids. "Birthdays are not news stories."

Min pulled a copy of a national newspaper from her backpack. The cover had an article about a woman turning seventy-three. She held it up in front of her with a *hmmf* sound.

"That's about the governor," I said. "It's a little different."

"Is the governor planning on having a whole petting zoo transported to her house and inviting everyone in Bear Creek?" Min crossed her arms. "Will the governor have an entire table of Marvelous Marmalade ice cream for her guests? I don't think so."

"Min, your birthday isn't news. And you should know that eleven is the age when people stop dotting their *i*'s with hearts."

Gloria burst out laughing, with Charlotte and Thom joining in. Even Min started to giggle. "Do you even know how to have fun, Nellie?" Min hiccupped, but it didn't sound at all the way it had when Alejandro had said it.

Just as we wrapped up the meeting, there was a soft knock on the barn doors. In came our families—Thom's parents (Sheila was holding a baby monitor), Mr. and Mrs. Kim-Franklin, Mom, Charlotte's dad, Chef Wells, Dr. Burke, and Gordon's dad. Gordon was the last to come in, his head down.

"I hope you don't mind the intrusion," Sheila said. "We were chatting in the kitchen and thought it best to bring our thoughts straight to all of you."

Dr. Burke sat down on the haystack across from me. "I have concerns about the Newspaper Club, but I also was quite impressed with how all of you handled yourselves at the school board meeting yesterday. Can we come up with some compromises? Some ground rules or expectations that we feel confident will keep all of you safe while also supporting your drive to share Bear Creek news?"

"No," I said.

But it was drowned out by everyone else in the club saying yes.

———————

"All stories should only be within a two-mile radius of town," Dr. Burke said. "Any farther, and you need a parent to accompany you."

"Five miles," I said.

"Three," she replied.

"Agreed."

On and on we bartered on points Dr. Burke brought up. In the end, we also agreed that the Cubs would never cover sources alone. We'd always let our parents know exactly where we were going. We'd meet sources at public places unless we knew them and had parental permission to visit them at their house. We would not take feral animals home with us. Basic stuff like that.

———————

That afternoon the Cubs crisscrossed town delivering our papers and then met at Wells Diner for a last-day-of-summer pizza.

Woodward was with me, so we ate at an outside table. Inside, Mom sat with Chef Wells and Mr. and Dr. Burke. Gordon's dad looked a lot like him—tall with a halfway smile.

Sheila was also there with Josie. Soon Charlotte's grandpa came in, too. He sat at a table with a bunch of older men. "He's been really quiet since I gave him and my parents the story I wrote about meeting Grandma," Charlotte said to me. "They keep having conversations in the library that they think I can't hear."

I let my mind skip over the fact that Charlotte had a library in her house. "Are you going to see Ms. Wilkonson soon?" I asked.

Charlotte nodded, a little smile on her face. "Hopefully next weekend. Mom's thinking about coming, too."

Gloria joined us when the line at the register petered out. "Dad's going to take over if anyone else comes in for the next few minutes," she said around a bite of pizza. "I'm beginning to wish we *had* hired a waitress after today's rush." She took another bite then said, "They broke up, by the way—my dad and the would-be waitress."

I eyed how close Mom was sitting to Chef Wells.

Gloria followed my eyes and laughed. "Don't worry. I don't think she's his type."

"Mom isn't dating, anyway." I mean, I didn't think she was. It was sort of like how Min told me not to burp and suddenly all I had thought about was burping, even though it wasn't at all in my mind a moment earlier.

Not that parental dating and burping were the same thing.

CHAPTER SEVENTEEN

"YOU DON'T NEED TO be scared. It's just school. Just a few hours. You'll be fine."

Woodward blinked at me and stretched in a patch of sunlight on the living room rug. Lucky cat.

"You know,"—I turned to Mom—"Thom is homeschooled. *I* am a fantastic candidate for homeschooling."

Mom sipped her coffee. "I have a book to write. Off you go."

I trudged to the curb. Min was there, wearing a kitten and rainbow backpack. I jerked the kitten keychain off my backpack and shoved it in a pocket. All of the worries that I hadn't been feeling about the first day of school slammed into me with each step toward the bus stop. *What if I got lost?* Step. *What if someone was mean to me?* Step. *What if my teacher hated me?* Step. *What if I wasn't smart enough?* Step. *What if no one would sit with me at lunch?* Step. *What if I burped a lot?* That was a new one. Thanks, Min.

Min danced in a circle so her flowered skirt swirled around her. How could she be so calm? "Aren't you nervous?" I asked her.

Min shook her head. "I'm smart, kind, and generally likeable. I'll be fine." She looked at me, scanning over my gray T-shirt, black shorts, gray sneakers. "Maybe you could smile. That might help you."

I reminded myself that I was named after Nellie Bly, a renowned journalist who suffered through admittance into an insane asylum to chronicle life there for her readers. Not that sixth grade was going to be like that. My heart thumped.

You've got to put yourself out there. I plastered a smile on my face.

"Less teeth. More of a tilt to the lips." Min beamed at me.

The bus rumbled down the road. I could do this. I could be brave. I could also dart across the street and hide in Thom's barn.

The doors to the bus opened in front of us. I patted my back pocket, making sure my notebook was there alongside a couple of pens. *Being brave doesn't mean you aren't scared, Nellie. It means you can be scared and do what you need to do anyway.*

I stepped onto the bus.

GLOSSARY

allude: to hint at or indirectly reference

budget: a list of articles planned for the next issue of a newspaper

ethics: a code of values and principles that guide a journalist's behavior. For example, a journalist would refuse a free gift because the gift could compromise or appear to compromise her impartiality.

fact-check: the act of checking factual information in newspaper articles to determine its truth and correctness

inherent bias: a previously held belief or value that affects how a news story is framed for readers

mock-up: a draft version of the newspaper used for editing

press conference: a meeting between a news source and the media, providing an opportunity for all involved journalists to ask their questions at one meeting versus many individual interviews

pull quotes: verbatim statements from sources that are highlighted in a news story

The Newspaper Club
CHECK YOUR FACTS

Have at least three independent checks for spellings
of every name, title and place.

SUBJECT	CHECK 1	CHECK 2	CHECK 3
Nellie Murrow	Student ID	Called Nellie to verify spelling	Checked spelling on press release

ACKNOWLEDGMENTS

Thank you to the best trio a writer can have—literary agent Nicole Resciniti, Running Press editor Julie Matysik, and senior publicity and marketing manager Val Howlett. Fact: Y'all are amazing. I'm so proud to be part of your team.

Much love also to illustrator Paula Franco, who perfectly captured all of the Cub reporters and brought their personalities to life.

Being able to work with the phenomenal Running Press crew is such a gift! Thank you, Marissa Raybuck, for the incredible and mindful cover and interior design. Project manager Amber Morris is the person I'm going to turn to during the zombie apocalypse—she knows exactly what should be happening and when and makes sure everyone else is on board. Copy editor Christina Palaia doesn't miss a wayward comma, overused word, forgotten detail, or opportunity to encourage. Vice president and associate publisher Jessica Schmidt's support is unmatched. Thank you doesn't begin to sum my gratitude to Running Press publisher Kristin Kiser. I don't know how I got to be so lucky to work with all of you!

Much gratitude also to the newspapers who solidified such a love for journalism in me—the *Daily Collegian,* the *Sharon Herald,* and the *York Daily Record/Sunday News.*

And lastly mentioned but first in my heart, thank you to my family and friends, especially Jon, Emma, and Ben.